leaving now

Caitlin Press Inc.
8100 Alderwood Road,
Halfmoon Bay, BC V0N 1Y1
www.caitlin-press.com

Edit by Anne-Marie Bennet
Text design by Vici Johnstone
Cover design by Pamela Cambiazo
Cover image by Arleigh Wood
Printed in Canada

Caitlin Press Inc. acknowledges financial support from the Government of Canada through the Canada Book Fund and the Canada Council for the Arts, and from the Province of British Columbia through the British Columbia Arts Council and the Book Publisher's Tax Credit.

Canada Council   Conseil des Arts
for the Arts   du Canada

BRITISH COLUMBIA
ARTS COUNCIL
We acknowledge the support of the Province of British Columbia
through the British Columbia Arts Council

Library and Archives Canada Cataloguing in Publication

Paré, Arleen

Leaving now / Arleen Paré.

ISBN 978-1-894759-74-8

I. Title.

PS8631.A7425L42 2012   C813'.6   C2012-900535-5

leaving now

Arleen Paré

July 2012
For marie —
In gay canadiarie
Enjoy — xt Arleen

CAITLIN PRESS

For Peter and Jesse

> *By three ways do we learn: first by reflection, which is the noblest; second by imitation, which is the easiest; third by experience, which is the bitterest.*
>
> — Confucius

Once Upon a Saturday

In the days before wholesale public recycling like we have now with blue boxes and paper separated out from glass jars and tin cans, in those days before general backyard composting, we put everything in a large trash can under the kitchen sink. We left it lidless, easier to toss things in, lined it with a green garbage bag, everything gathering together, sliding down the plastic walls, settling.

Every week I put out two green garbage bags. Hefted them to the back lane in my nightgown with the red poncho overtop so I looked okay for the neighbours in the maybe two inches of snow in late March that year. Our first house, first year in Vancouver, on the edge of the Pacific.

Our block rowed twenty houses, ten on the north side and ten on the south, stucco and wood siding, side by side, fenced or hedged or open to the road. In the back lanes each household left two giant plastic bags of garbage every week. So much garbage in the back lanes those days, a municipal garbage strike could ruin a neighbourhood in under two weeks.

So much garbage you could go through a neighbour's trash and know in minutes how your neighbour lived. Reach in, urban archaeologist; pull out one item at a time, place one item beside another:

a child's drawing of a blue-crayoned house, crumpled;

an empty Noxema jar;

banana peels;

flashlight batteries;

eggshells;

a hand-knit mitten unravelling at the thumb.

Arrange each article on a table, trying to make a pattern, expecting apple pie, recreating days before, weeks before, a kind of ordinary before, before everything went off the rails. Before the fairytale begins.

Listen. Voices ricochet inside this place, this place that's like a midden, morning sounds, this last Saturday in June.

Whose voices could I bear to hear? Whose tongues lapped round the *Morning, mornings,* and the milky grains, and orange juice from a plastic jug? I swirled it round before I poured. It sat like bile all night the night before, inside those plastic walls, separating. Who slept? What news this Saturday would bring. The smell of cut grass, a lawn mower in the yard next door, the radio, refrigerator thrum, a dog barking behind a neighbour's fence, spilled milk, and acid, yellow in the yellow jug.

The plain suburban sun threw shadows on the door out front, the curtains in the den spread wide to lacy shrubs, the pebbled yard, the cedar hedge. Rays dappled across the threshold onto the kitchen floor, the pile of bones, garbage scraps, the site.

This is just a kitchen, a burial mound inside one version of suburban life: 1980 west-coast, middle-class-domestic. What could be more plain?

There are no formal notes. Decades pass. All that's left is digging through the human cells. Brushing off the sound of thunder. No official transcripts. No photos taken of the day or of the door. No sacred marks painted to protect the threshold or the family. No tears left beneath fine particles of light. It was a Saturday. An ordinary day — but with a suitcase in it.

Paré

I rose at seven that morning and started collecting clothes and books and bathroom things. Not all my clothes or all my books, just enough for a couple of nights, stuffing them into a suitcase which was part of a luggage set that his parents gave me nine Christmases earlier, and which I had interpreted at the time to be a sign they didn't really want me in the family. A sign that if I crammed everything I owned into that matching set of tan-coloured suitcases, sized to fit inside each other like a set of Russian dolls, the way years nest inside us, that if I packed up my belongings and left, his parents would not have interrupted their pre-dinner rum and cokes to wave good-bye. The way it used to be said that the gift of soap meant the receiver needed a good wash, the gift of luggage suggested leaving. Sensitive to signs, I was hurt they might not want me anymore. But it wasn't that at all. It was just a Christmas gift.

I was packing for the weekend, but I was also leaving for good. I'd be gone from the way it was, forever. The way it was in our house, us all together, would be gone. I left most things behind, because our new arrangement meant that I'd be back in three days, taking turns with him every other week to be with the kids. Which made it less like leaving. But it was leaving anyway. I took the two books I was reading, but I left the others on the shelf.

After I zipped up the suitcase, I shuffled to the kitchen. Stopped at the threshold, dropped the bag, the floor heaving, the middle of the kitchen collapsing in on itself. The countertop buckled and the milk carton slipped to the edge, tipped over. Milk sloshed everywhere. The dishwasher door clunked open like a medieval drawbridge. Two plates cracked and the faucet started running. The stove light popped. Then the phone rang and it was him. He'd stayed at her place overnight, and he said, I'm going to bring her over.

You mean right now, I said, while I'm still here. The kitchen settled down.

We'll be there in twenty minutes, he answered.

It doesn't make sense, I told him. Or did I say, It doesn't matter.

I said, tightening my grip on the receiver, No, don't bring her over. But he did anyway.

The kids turned on the Saturday morning cartoons and watched Popeye and the first half of Rocky the Flying Squirrel before they raced up from the basement where the TV lived. They poured Cheerios into their bowls and orange juice into their glasses, and on the way back downstairs they peeked into our bedroom where I was making the bed, and asked: Where's Dad, and I said, He'll be home in twenty minutes. So they rushed downstairs again, cereal bowls and juice glasses in hand, to catch the end of Rocky the Flying Squirrel. They hadn't even noticed my suitcase at the door.

Some people think kids know everything on some intuitive level, but later that morning when I told them I was leaving, their faces crumpled, innocent, unprotected as unbuttered toast.

The 1980 sun carved shadows in the yard out front. The cedar hedge kept rusting in its place. Morning, with afternoon behind it, engulfed the hallway floor, the kitchen door. A jam jar collared daisies stiff with past and a wishbone paled on the windowsill. A two-quart carton had drained itself of milk. Loose pages from the weekend news: the twenty-eighth of June. School year just ended, it should have been a bird-song day. Should have been no story, no fairytale, no talk of bones, no whispers underneath the kitchen sink.

A Long Long Time Ago

Shake this sieve   sift the years   fragments of first teeth and chips of bone from chil-
dren's wrists   chips of terra cotta mugs   sift sand from shoes and sand from garden
gloves   eggshell shards   a line of cookie crumbs   toss leftover salt over the left shoul-
der   then the right   sweat shining on an upper lip   find a ring that vanished   a piece
of string   a coil from a small Nintendo game

At twenty-one, I married him. I was pregnant. He was twenty-three. Two weeks before the wedding we huddled over my parents' kitchen table after lunch, not knowing what to say to each other. Soda crackers crumbed our plates. Sanka cooled in our abandoned mugs. He took my right hand and studied it, almost a romantic gesture. Then he looked into my eyes, still holding my hand in his, and said: Your fingers look exactly like Polaris missiles; your knuckles ... I yanked my hand back into my lap, tears damming my eyes. I fought them hard. That he thought my fingers looked like Polaris missiles was not a good sign.

In 1967, everyone knew about Polaris missiles, which had been deployed a few years earlier against Cuba in the Bay of Pigs incident. Ballistic weaponry named after the North Star. I remember sitting at my grade eleven desk, the Bay of Pigs discussed in class, we knew it signalled the beginning of the end. America vulnerable for the first time.

What do you mean? I asked him, my errant knuckles hiding in my lap.

Nothing, just interesting how your fingers bulge at the knuckles, the same way Polaris missiles are shaped. He tried to pry my hand from below the tabletop. Thick at the middle. Sensing his mistake, he shook his head. It's not bad, he said, just interesting.

Later, when I told his sister about the Polaris missile incident, she said, don't worry, he's a good person, he has a good sense of humour, and I decided to believe her, because she knew him better than I did. And because in two weeks we were getting married. It was like an arranged marriage — we had so little chance to make up our minds, to choose. It was that prescribed.

I cried a lot those months. In front of, and behind my eyes. Crying was a side effect. Two weeks before the wedding I went to his parent's house for dinner with his whole family, nine kids, two parents and Penny, their German shepherd cross. Except the oldest daughter wasn't there. She was in California with her own first baby. Halfway through dinner, I leaned over and said, Excuse me, to his mother who sat beside me, I need to use the washroom. With so many people around the table, no one else paid much attention. She pointed the way. The dog followed me to the powder room adjacent to the vestibule and waited outside as I threw up lasagne for five whole minutes. Another side effect.

Nothing stayed down. They called it morning sickness, but I threw up morning, noon, and night. I threw up on my way to work at 8:00 a.m., walking through the Canadian Pacific train station. In the classroom, saying to the grade four boys, Carry on with the math questions on page 44; I'll be back in five. The school bathroom just across the hall. Driving in the car with him along the winter roads, I kept the window down.

Twenty-four hours before the wedding my mother drove me to a doctor in Pointe Claire for pills to keep me from throwing up on the way to the altar. I lost a lot of weight: on my wedding day I weighed in at 108.

The day my son was born I worried about those pills. I had swallowed them for seven months, as long as I was morning sick. Toward the end of pregnancy, I learned that thalidomide, a pill which deformed the limbs of newborns, had been prescribed for morning sickness too. When I saw my newborn son, I counted his fingers, soft and pink as buds, all ten, no bulges at the middle.

Despite the pills and my Polaris knuckles, things were going better than expected. I learned that the early Greeks referred to Polaris, the polestar, as the Pillar of Heaven. My lucky star, my first-born was born intact. My fingers bulged in the middle, but they were now classic and celestial.

Is it true he never said he loved me? In all our years together, did he never say he loved me? Maybe he did, but if he did, he never said it first. Before we were married, before I was pregnant, he said, let's get married in two years. Driving home from a friend's wedding (our friend hardly showed at all), inspired, he hunched over the steering wheel of his Volkswagen bug shimmying along the icy 2 and 20, cleared his throat and repeated, let's get married. Shifted gears. When I finish medical school, keeping his eyes on the slick white highway. In two years, though my first love will always be medicine. Keeping his eyes strictly on the frosty road.

I was flattered and not flattered. I had been drinking; it was a wedding. I thought: married to a doctor. I thought: and always come second. But he had a sexy upper lip shaped like an archer's bow. He was shy, but filled at the same time with a confidence that comes from comfort. It made him appealing. His family was appealing too. Two years and to tell the truth I didn't know what medicine-as-a-first-love meant. Maybe he was wrong about who or what would come first. I had nothing else in mind at the time, and teaching grade four boys, I'd hoped, was only a stop on the way to something more important.

So I said: Yes. And would you mind stopping the car, I have to pee. He pulled over onto the crunchy shoulder and I peed in the frozen bushes at the side of the highway. It was after midnight — two trucks flashed by. Shivering in my high heels and miniskirt, I rushed back to the car. Burrs festooned the ankles of my diaphanous pantyhose, shiny, white as the road. I peeled them off, my pantyhose, cranked down the tiny VW window, and released them into the November wind. Bye-bye, white stockings. I waved after them. We watched them in the rear-view, fluttering like a leggy ghost down the highway.

Right then he should have said he loved me. It was called for in that moment. It's possible he didn't know how to say I love you. It's possible I didn't know how to understand I love you without it being said.

My mother told my father I was pregnant, which was how we told my father anything important in our house. Grinning later, his hands in his trouser pockets, he said to me: I guess I'll have to get my shotgun. Which was how he told me that he knew, and how he told me he wasn't mad. After all, I was marrying a doctor.

The wedding day was January 6, the Feast of Epiphany, which had just been demoted from its former status as a Holy Day, freeing it up for things like weddings. It was January, so I wore a velvet dress. But sleeveless.

I'll freeze, I complained to the dressmaker and my mother who huddled together over the McColl's pattern that showed a sketch of a blond in a simple panelled dress with sleeves. Thin, in a pillbox hat.

No, no, these sleeves are all wrong for you, you must wear sleeveless, said the dressmaker. She was adamant. Sleeveless is very slimming, she said. My mother agreed. It's easy to make this dress without the sleeves. They nodded together. It was 1968.

You're short, said the dressmaker, like your mother, looking my mother up and down. Like me, she allowed. She stood back; she was shorter than either of us. Believe me, I've seen plenty, she said, warming to her subject, sleeveless suits us shorties. My mother agreed with the dressmaker that even at 108 pounds, even in forty-below weather, slimmer was the priority.

I walked up the aisle, nausea-free and sleeveless, my father cupping my goose-bumped elbow, angled so I could hold the bouquet of gardenia and stephanotis. The white velvet draped over my flat belly as though nothing was there after all. Following the ceremony, after signing the register, after thanking Father Leblanc, who used to hear my confessions, after taking my new husband's arm, after whisking down the aisle, I threaded my cold blotchy arms through the fat furry sleeves of a white bunny jacket, rented for the occasion. The official photographer clicked us perched and grinning in the back seat of the white limousine, engine running, just before we left for the reception at the Airport Skyline Hotel.

The reception featured a receiving line and speeches and toasts, everyone clinking glasses. A fairytale wedding with a Baked Alaska parade, waiters bearing the ice cream confection aloft around the dining room, then returning to the kitchen to slice and serve before it melted on the serving trays.

My groom nodded shyly in his rented Prince Charming morning suit with a dove-grey vest. He looked as handsome as a movie star. The guests smiled approvingly despite the shocking cold that day, despite the fact that the bride was pregnant and her knuckles resembled Polaris missiles, though most of them would not have noticed the resemblance.

My new husband, so young and unpractised, made his speech, which hinged on an amusing story about my grandmother.

This is a story about Daisy, he said to the friendly crowd. She told me this herself a couple of days ago. Though a story of betrayal, it counted as romantic. An Irish fairytale. My grandmother had discovered my grandfather's Hibernian sash in his wedding trunk when she unpacked it on their wedding night, December 1899. He had promised her that he was *not, absolutely not,* a member of the Hibernians, that Irish rebel sect which had been condemned from the pulpit by my grandmother's parish priest. She had called off her earlier engagement to a beau of seven years, Patrick Heaney, solely because Patrick Heaney *was* an admitted member of the Hibernians, and would not agree to leave the sect. Not even for her.

When my grandmother found my grandfather's sash folded at the bottom of his trunk, it was too late. He had lied to her, but she was already married to him, which made it strangely romantic.

Everybody laughed, the humour of hindsight, what love will do. My grandmother sat at the table to our left behind her Coke-bottle glasses, smiling and frail, the centre of attention. She was in her late eighties then; her Hibernian husband had died four years earlier. She had not forgotten about the sash. She had told my husband all about it. It was the centre of her life.

She leaned back in her chair and twiddled her thumbs, a thing you don't see much anymore, hands folded in her lap. She rested her big knuckles over her blue wool bulge of a tummy, thumbs falling over each other like tumblers in a lock, keeping her company.

After the reception at the Skyline, I tossed the stephanotis. We changed into travel clothes and drove the VW north along the Auto Route into the Laurentians for our forty-below honeymoon at his family's country cottage. We drank champagne that night, which his parents had left for us in the fridge. We cranked up the heat and ate Triscuits and brie.

The next day the VW wouldn't start. Under the mint-green hood, the battery lay frozen as an iceberg.

I don't recall the first time I felt the give in the floor as I stepped across that scuffed square-foot of lino near the sink. I thought nothing of it. I was racing around too fast to pay attention, even to weird things. Especially to weird things. Maybe I was rushing out to pick up the kids from soccer, running late. Or maybe I needed to buy ice cream for dessert, running late.

But I remember when it really began to bother me. It was months before I left. Lunging from the fridge to the stove with the milk for the mashed potatoes, I almost toppled, almost spilled the milk, the lino was so spongy at that moment. I dashed milk into the pot and kept mashing, mulling over my misstep, thinking I must have imagined it. But when my oldest swung through the back door, edging it open with his shoulder, carrying a pile of comic books in his arms, hair in his eyes, I said, hey, check out the floor here, pointing with my foot. No, right here. He dropped the comic books onto the table, stepped over to the sink and tapped his foot over the spot.

Feel spongy to you?

Nope, he answered with no hesitation, not spongy.

Sure? I asked.

He nodded sure, throwing his jacket on a chair.

What's for dinner? Looking in the fridge.

Pork chops.

Dessert?

Ice cream. Chocolate chip.

Reassured, he thumped down the basement stairs two at a time to catch the end of *Charlie's Angels*. I knelt on the floor and pressed the palm of my hand over the space. Nothing. I pressed harder to force a yield, even a little. But the floor refused. No give whatsoever, solid as slate, but with a slight, very slight depression, if I squinted. Which is when I remembered that I'd noticed it before.

In any fairytale the mother is gone:

        gone-missing

           gone-bad

              gone-off-the-rails

           gone-for-the-afternoon

      gone-crazy

           gone-fishing

                gone-sour

           gone-to-drink

      gone-shopping

      gone-to-the-dogs

        gone-to-ground

     definitely gone   gone-gone

           gone forever

     gone for now

        gone-off-with-another-man

     died-and-gone

     gone-to-sleep-for-ten-minutes

   gone-to sleep-for-the-night

      gone-to-the-big-house

          up-and-gone

      gone-off-with-another-woman

           gone-to-school

  gone-to-work

      gone-to-hell-in-a-hand basket

According to technical definitions, fairytales feature fairies, goblins, elves, trolls, giants, gnomes, magic and enchantments. Often the fairytale contains farfetched events. And while the term fairytale sounds promising, as in a fairytale ending, not all fairytales end happily. Not for everyone.

A fairytale contains a lesson.

In a fairytale the mother is almost always absent, missing from the action.

In this fairytale I am the mother. I am not yet absent; the story has not yet begun. Neither fairies nor ogres have appeared. I still boil hot dogs for my boys' lunches, smooth mustard and sea-green relish onto hot dog buns, pour whole milk into their pirate glasses. I still fold pairs of socks, grey with navy heels, and navy with heels of grey. I make up their beds with cotton sheets patterned with knights and castles in the clouds. At bedtime I read to them, though they can read, I tuck them into bed.

Another woman can enter the fairytale to replace the missing mother, but replacements are not the real thing; replacements do not save a child from story.
Story is about the fact of gone. Gone-real-gone.

A real real-there mother protects a child from story, which is always a bad story; bad things always happen in a story. In any fairytale, bad things will happen.

I became the gone-off-the-rails kind of gone-mother, gone-off-the-straight-and-narrow-rails, gone-off-with-another-woman.

Later I became the gone-from-the-day-to-day gone kind of mother.

My replacement suntanned in the backyard that last Saturday in June, lying on a blanket the size of a fridge door, reading a magazine. We could see her from the kitchen. She was trying to get a tan, trying to stay clear of the mess inside the house that day, waiting for the mess to settle, waiting for her entrance cue. For the story to begin.

He brought her over anyway that morning and she lay on a blanket in our backyard in a rectangle of sun reading a magazine and waiting for the real real-gone mother to leave. Which I would do, and also not do. We could see her from the kitchen window.

His new girlfriend.

No one should have to cry; it is such violence to eyes. Save the tears, things can always get worse. And this room in the middle of everything is just a room overlooking the deck and backyard. Just a burial site, a small indoor midden with the regular array. Kitchen scraps, carcasses of chickens, peelings, apples and oranges, fish tails, empty tins, broken shells. A room with a sliding glass door, grumble and thunder inside its grooves.

Some days I kneel by the pile, the burial site in the middle of things, pick up a bone. The leg bone of a human, a female. Hold it up to the light. By the length you can see it's the femur of a woman of child-bearing age, maybe thirty-two, thirty-three. By the angle you can see she is walking out the door.

Then One Day

. . . in a universe incommensurate with this one.
— Elizabeth Bishop

the August night febrile as fireworks they were playing disco at the club a women's bar we didn't know when she

she somehow
she tilted her head her shoulder
something she did something which

flipped me I don't know a double-flip inside a central chakra tectonic plates slip-sliding underneath my ribs the impact geological my bony cage unhinging I almost heard the whoosh-sub-whoosh beneath the earth's crust cracking the endless disco beat the heat the sudden sharpest want bigger space unexpected like a curtain loosened falling the heat inside the club a women's club we didn't really know the music thumping one hundred women more neon-white against the purple shadows hips dipping pulling close their blinding summer neon jeans that shocking black light orchid-white the non-stop pulse a night-time sweat-line beading on my upper lip seeing her her tilting face her shrugging hips

my eyes first time full light belly too like curtains their daytime loops loosened undone

Earlier that day, the four of us, my sister-in-law and the other two women who were my sister's friends from Ottawa. Slip-sliding down the trail to Wreck Beach. My sister-in-law didn't know the other two women, not really, but she wanted to go with us to Wreck Beach.

First time for us to go to Wreck Beach, a nude beach. All those suntanned bodies, suntanned all over, no clothes at all. My sister-in-law and I taped band-aids over our nipples against the hot August sun, which made the others laugh, oiled-up and fearless. Those summer days, the seventies, before the sun turned nasty in the sky.

That night then, agreeing to meet the other two at the women's club we didn't know, dancing just for fun. We liked dancing. Dressing up after supper, my sister-in-law and I, to meet the other two. Our kids, my boys and their cousin, playing in the basement, and our husbands playing backgammon, which they liked that summer.

That night when I got home I could not pull the curtain closed against the night, the open-wide revealing everything I'd need to know.
Nothing ever the same again.

Paré

Too hot, the night became a Catherine Wheel.
The music unstopping and my sister-in-law
bobbing safe, alone, beside us, dancing like a hippy.
Our husbands safe at home
with backgammon, which they preferred.

The heat that night unsafe.   Laws
and plain relationships not playing by the rules.
They were at home with the coffee table.
We wore band-aids on our nipples at the beach.
They played backgammon.

Magenta
kindled on her face, her hands that night,
her mouth stained shocking white,
her hips black lit, her eyes

                         were the eyes of a malamute.
She was the first, she didn't last, she was a door,
a one-way path, a door that opened out, out only.

Where is the sorrow?   All the rooms are lit with sun and cloud.   All rooms bear down. Where are the children?   The morning table is set with an oilcloth.   Red with black squares in the middle.   Morning presses.   Where are the children?   Sitting in the basement.   The TV is lit.   Listening to TV's timelessness.   The cartoon squirrel flies into the horizon.   Sky fades.   Morning presses down.

The next day I called her from my office, from my part-time Family Counselling desk, recalling her shoulder, her tilting head, her smile, magenta lit. She was staying in Vancouver for the summer, and love, unexpected, had fallen over me, a sudden August rain. I called her up. Opened up my lap. My mouth. It was not a planning thing. I did not think through the next three seasons, rain and sun and wind. Fall and winter, and then the spring.

The sudden lip of next year's summer. The unexpected weight of ten months falling on the end of June, the leaving day.

First and second principles. First principle: how could I stay? Second principle: how could I not?

The seventies: those mythic days of liberation. Momentum from the 1960s, the iconic golden age, those years of roller-coaster break-neck change. Landing on the moon. Small step, big step. Everybody worshipping the petals on the flowers. The sixties, their sacred space, the public buzz.

Those decades. It would have been unprincipled not to notice, to wear no daisies in your hair, the whole world surging forward: civil rights, students' rights, free love, the sexual revolution, freedom, freedom, open marriage, save the planet, save the whales, black pride, gay pride, save the giant redwoods, stop the war, stop the capitalist pig dog propaganda, the nuclear family, the nuclear bomb.

My youngest later told me, you were doing your own thing, Mum. In part, I guess I was. The thing women were doing in towns and on radio shows and on TV, in magazines and dailies, on campuses, in offices and factories. Everywhere. Everyone doing, dancing, liberating ourselves, the streets, the books, the bras. Marching marches. Sit-ins, be-ins, love-ins. Revolutionary exhortations: *Drop out. Steal this book. Burn this draft card. Wear flowers in your hair. Make love not war.* Stonewall. Four dead at Kent State. Letter bombs in Montreal. Any woman can. The energy swept through kitchens, bedrooms, bus stops. Riots in the cities. Women's liberation, protests and grape boycotts, love beads and hookahs, acid and god's-eyes, acid rain, the Pill. Drugs-sex-rock-and-roll. Re-invention of the Western world. Answers in the wind, in blades of grass, blowing, a hundred miles an hour.

When I walked down the lane behind my stucco house, I clicked my heels together, clacking in mid-air. I was Dorothy, I was the Wizard. Trees rustled their taffeta skirts in my direction. Sparrows pitched Broadway tunes into cloudless skies. The sun threw rhinestones onto all the kitchen windows.

Is this too naive, too earnest? Who can afford earnestness in this runaway world? No one wants that kind of trouble now. No one wants to hear about revolution or sharing wealth, or the possibility of light or flowers in someone else's hair, about redwoods growing thick as houses in suburban tracts. Or about a time ago when women were the heroes, fomenting insurrection in the laundromats, becoming lovers in the streets, committing changes and delinquencies. Kissing in old cars, holding hands in movie theatres or under night-time eaves.

dancing carefree as a sprung floor when she shrugged her shoulder   the neon light   the
sudden lust
like most lust   which is to say   one minute you're dancing or smoking a cigarette or
getting off a bus   and the next minute   the next minute is suddenly ballooning   your
eyes have never really seen before

I never knew   I said to her that night
a secret   she placed her finger on my lips   a trick they do with mirrors   to keep us
from each other

hard then not to notice   everywhere I went   women   to keep both hands over my
two eyes

she did not last
which is to say

another woman   and then another

Once Upon A Time . . . Again

The day I told my youngest, he said, oh no, a gaylord. We had stopped for a red light. Only ten years old but still he knew to say, oh no, a gaylord. It was early March. I was driving him from school to the dentist, north along the Kingsway.

Does it mean eating out at home? he asked after a while. He was trapped; he couldn't open the car door in the middle of Tuesday afternoon traffic and on the way out, say: I don't want to hear anything more about your weirdo-gaylord-lifestyle. So he asked his question, belted into the passenger seat, his eyes barely able to see out over the dashboard.

Lesbian, I said, the word is lesbian, not gaylord. I didn't know what to say about eating-out-at-home. Clearly he learned more at school than long division. The light turned green. I told him about his tutor, who was also a lesbian and about my sister, his aunt who lived in Ottawa, and three of my friends he already knew. In those days I thought it was important to tell as much as possible. A form of confession maybe. I passed a car on my right. The windows sluiced with rain. Thinking giving more facts meant I was being helpful, like more information would make it more okay. We looked ahead through the rhythm of the windshield wipers. All along the Kingsway, the swish of those syncopated wipers. He asked, If you got together with your sister, Mum, would you be sisbians?

I told him in the car that day, not because I'd planned to, but because he had just then said, you need a boyfriend, Mum. Dad has a girlfriend. Which he knew because his Dad had stayed at the girlfriend's house the night before. It was a practical suggestion, with equality in mind. But I said, No, no boyfriend, honey, I'm more interested in women now. Which was when he slapped the heel of his hand to his forehead and said, Oh no, a gaylord. A schoolyard word.

I told my oldest that night at dinnertime. He looked up from his dinner, his fork stopping halfway to his mouth, But isn't that a problem, Mum?

What do you mean, a problem? I said.

It's in the book, he told me, as though I already knew. Both kids scrambled from the table returning with *The Joy of Sex* from a high-up bookshelf in the study. Ten and twelve, and they had read *The Joy of Sex*. Memorized it. My oldest flipped through the pages towards the end of the book. He pointed to where it said lesbian sex was a problem. Just one page at the end of the book, an afterthought, describing it as a problem.

A problem for men, maybe, but not for me, I said, and closed the book. They weren't men yet, but already they'd read that it was a problem for a woman to love another woman. They could tell I was mad, but not at them. They couldn't figure it out and they didn't ask and I couldn't think of how to explain the kind of problem *The Joy of Sex* thought it was.

We finished the leftover chicken à la king. Their Dad was away at a conference. He was away a lot that spring. We talked about what I had told my youngest in the car on the way to the dentist, the details, so we were all in the same loop. We talked about the dentist and how my youngest fell asleep in the dentist's chair that afternoon. He always fell asleep in the dentist's chair.

When I tucked them in after stories, I didn't know what to say about the dinner conversation, how to sum it up, make it more normal. They asked no more questions either.

I tidied the kitchen and found a tiny mirror on the kitchen counter, the size of flattened pea. Strange, but life is. I slipped it into my jeans' pocket, alongside the train-flattened penny the kids gave me years ago. For luck.

I'm having an affair with a woman, I said as we drove through the intersection at Twelfth and MacDonald. I thought you should know. Driving home from a French restaurant, ten months before I left, celebrating my thirty-third birthday with rabbit kidneys in brandy cream sauce, a bottle of St. Emillion and chocolate mousse, and as I steered the car along McDonald, I said, I've started an affair with a woman. Street lights flashing by overhead. I couldn't look at him. Another block and then another.

Finally he said, I guess I'll have to treat it like any other affair. And I thought: what any other affair? But I said nothing. Though now I think maybe he was just trying to be fair, reasonable, not going crazy about me having an affair with a woman. I didn't know what he was thinking and I didn't know what to say. I just kept driving along the night-time suburban streets through the pale-green sodium light: right turn, left, left again, then straight along for ten blocks, right turn into the back lane, left into the carport. Home.

Where is the father?   On his way.   With black squares in the middle.   The sky fades. Where are the women?   Writing.   Families fade.   The bowls are blue and the cloth is red with black in the centre.   The children are in the basement.   The TV lights their faces blue.   The fear is not anticipated.   Gradually.   Time presses.   Half time and half not time.   Half for now and half for the rest of their lives.   Hope fades.   Morning presses down.

A few months after *I'll have to treat it like any other affair*, after the unravelling began, which it did, stitch by stitch, day by day — later, in another French restaurant on the other side of town, maybe it was our anniversary, January, it would have been our twelfth — me crying over a plate of watercress soup, watching the swirl of cream lose its perfect coil as I pressed the back of the spoon through the soup's glossy surface, letting the green paleness seep into the spoon's silver bowl. I watched the soup fill the spoon. I couldn't eat it. I couldn't swallow anything. I placed the spoon on the plate below the bowl, soundlessly. The soup cooled, the waiter removed the soup without comment.

Waiters must see this all the time, husbands and wives. We had to change the subject, something remote and impersonal, any closeness seeping out, a pale coolness shrinking the air around us.

Paré

I dream about my youngest son. He steps off a train with a flock of other children just short of the station platform, because the station for some reason cannot accommodate this train. An adult, who is his own grown-up self, carries him to the platform where we wait for him with our arms outstretched, but when his adult self places his child self on the platform, the child self runs away. He has run away once or twice before, so we think: well, of course. But still the panic rises. I ask the station master to stop the trains and he does, in the interest of safety. But my son is gone and I don't know how to get him back.

When I wake up I know what I will have to do. I will enter the forest behind the train station and sing to him: I need you to come back; my arms will cry without you. I am not a singer, but I will sing it for him. Until he walks back into my arms.

To forget: to lose the remembrance of; to cease to think of (forgive and forget).

To forgive: to cease to feel angry or resentful towards; to pardon (an offender, offence).

Trials of exactitude: trying to calculate gradations, layers, linguistics of despair. Which word applies. To this situation.

To mend: to restore to sound condition; repair; heal.

Paré

I spooned love words into their baby mouths;
their elfin forms, beloved and unknown.

No doors lead out of history. Or out of mother love.
Read tea leaves, check the maps.

My children memorized my palms.
They tolerate the story's arc.

I roll out mistakes like dice;
stare down the past, as if

risk will prove my adoration,
illuminate the riddle. Mother. Child. Fortune. Love.

Every night before bedtime, their post-bath heads, damp young muskrats, rested against my shoulders, their small bodies crowding my sides to see the pictures, follow the pages. I read them bedtime stories, books and books: *In the Night Kitchen, The Elephant and the Bad Baby, Hansel and Gretel, Pokey Little Puppy, The Hobbit. Babar,* where on the final page the elephant mothers follow Babar's new car, forced to hold up their trunks to avoid breathing in the dust. Each book, over and over.

Sometimes, if we knew the book inside-out and backwards, I'd change a word here or there to liven up the reading just for fun. But they always lifted their knowing heads and fixed me with that look that meant *don't mess with the story, Mum.*

Library books, gift books, books that appeared out of nowhere. Their cheeks bright as stoplights from the steaming bath. Their stillness for the page, the pages turning one by one to the end. Their beautiful butterfly ears. Everything on the sofa hushed, every part of them attuned to the story.

When I went to bed, I read Dr. Spock. Later I read *Sisterhood Is Powerful, Of Woman Born, The Female Eunuch.*

When he was in bed beside me, though sometimes he wasn't, sometimes he was on an overnight rotation at the hospital saving lives, but when he was in bed beside me, he read *The New England Journal of Medicine.* Sometimes he read *The Lancet.*

When we were first married, we read to each other at bedtime, an ordinary romantic practice, a sweet one. We read *Till We Have Faces* by C.S. Lewis. We were twenty-one and twenty-three, our faces still more innocent than not.

Paré

Guilt: the fact of having committed a specified or implied offence; culpability; the feeling of this.

Regret: a feeling of sorrow, repentance, disappointment over an action or loss.

Remorse: deep regret for a wrong committed.

The restlessness these words can cause.

Maybe I take liberties, making public what should be kept inside the house, behind doors, underneath the floorboards and the lino tiles. I am ashamed. Of course. No longer can belong. Ashamed also of the shame. Ashamed of the guilt. This indulgence.

Maybe I embellish. Growing maudlin, filling with remorse. Worrying this flattened penny, this tiny mirror. This guilty business of the state of guilt. Ashamed of writing it out loud. But writing.

When the boys brought their empty cereal bowls back to the kitchen that last Saturday in June, they sat with me at the table where I was eating toast and peanut butter. They played a game on a small hand-held computer where cartoon babies kept falling from a burning building. They tried to save the babies, tried to press the right key in time before the babies landed on the sidewalk. Grabbing the game from each other. Cascading babies, flames leaping up in animated loops. I watched them as they grabbed it from each other, back and forth like a tennis game. They were ten and almost twelve.

They knew nothing about what was going to happen, though the past year had been a strange one. The oldest put on weight, a layer of fat against hard times. The youngest ran away one day after school for a couple of hours. It made me frantic, the tacit sadness of it.

Kindness to Strangers

Morning presses on us.   All weight.   All press.   All except the timeless time at the opening of the eyelids.   The moment before the clock radio starts.   All weight.   All except a slit when the eyes flit open, the split second before time is no longer timeless. All weigh down.   All press.   Except the slivered piece, one second before the time takes over.   All press down.   Except the timeless time before the day begins.   Morning presses on us.   Where is the sorrow?   All the rooms are lit with sun and cloud. All rooms bear down.   Where are the children?   The morning table is set with an oilcloth.   Red with a square of black squares in the middle.   Morning presses down. Where are the children?   Sitting in the basement.   The TV is lit.   Listening to timelessness.   Keeping family in the timelessness of time.   The cartoon squirrel flies into the horizon.   The sky fades.   Morning presses down.   Where is the father?   On his way.   With black squares in the middle.   Red oilcloth with black in the middle.   The sky fades.   Where are the women?   Writing.   Women are writing and the families fade.   The bowls are blue, the cloth is red with black in the centre.   The children are in the basement.   The TV lights their faces blue.   The fear is not anticipated.   Gradually. Time presses.   Half time and half not time.   Half for now and half for the rest of their lives.   The morning presses.   Where are the children of the children?   Waiting.   The past is moving away.   Boundaries are fading and boundaries are forming.   The table is set.   The tablecloth is red and blue bowls rest upon it.   Morning presses down.   All weight.   This morning.   This morning presses on us.   Where is the mother?   Fading from the morning.   Women are writing.   With black in the middle.   One bowl is cracked.   With spoons at the sides.   All this is for the time when the children ascend the stairs.   The cracks do not fade.   Cereal boxes stand on the table.   Lit with halfsun.   Half-cloud is on the table too.   Half the cloth lights with half-sun.   With spoons upon it.   Stainless steel half-fills with glint.   The minutes float.   When the time will come.   The morning presses down.   Where is the guilt?   At the side.   With white light in the bowls of the spoons.   The house is fading.   The children rise into halfsunshine.   And their faces half-fade.   Morning presses.   Where are the words?   In their mother's mouth.   There is half-sun and half is cloud.   All come together.   All split apart.   Morning presses down.   The red is the oilcloth and the black is on the red. The bowls are on the edge and the black is in the middle.   There is fading.   There is black in the middle.

You look like brother and sister, people told us, even strangers at parties, nodding, pleased with themselves. We both had mid-brown hair and brown eyes and rosy complexions, which made us look alike and as common as two house sparrows.

We were unalike too. He was reasonable; he valued reasonableness. He didn't know how to manage my goofiness, my edginess. If I could make myself sound reasonable, keep my feelings out of sight, conversations worked better. I didn't object to his reasonableness. But sometimes it was hard to keep my feelings out of sight.

I wanted us to be more alike, more equal. How about we both work part-time, I said to him; that would be fair, take turns staying home with the kids. That kind of equal. But he replied, When you can earn as much as me. Which was not the kind of equal I had in mind.

I wanted to know him better too, but he claimed I already knew him.

What you see is what you get, he said. There's nothing more. But I don't even know your favourite colour, I said, which I thought was uncomplicated. Everyone has a favourite colour.

Why do you have to know my favourite colour, he accused me, if I don't have one?

When we first met I asked him, what does it mean when they say God is love. Never could figure that one out. In those days those things mattered to me.

What do you want from me, he asked, answers?

Sure, I wanted answers if he had them, but more than that I think I wanted connection, a little conversation.

Barren is an old-fashioned word. As in, I'm barren, which is what I said to myself about my twenty-year-old body whenever I considered birth control. The Pill was new, and barren was old-fashioned and abstract, more a state of mind, like immortality or destiny, than a matter of flesh and blood. Which was the point.

Despite my abstract state of mind, I recall the exact moment I knew I was pregnant. A small key turned somewhere below my belly, locks and tumblers falling into place. I was heading home from his downtown student apartment, waiting for the traffic light to change at Peel and Sherbrooke, walking south to the CPR station to catch the train home to my house, my parents' house, after a weekend in town. The Sunday afternoon sharp with November grit and just before the traffic light turned green, before I stepped off the sidewalk, something inside me clicked. I was pregnant.

I knew. No one stood beside me, so there was no one I could tell. And even though I recognized the precise moment inside my body, the exact moment of fertilization, later I could not believe it. The word pregnant, concrete and visceral, did not fit with the word barren, which is an abstract state of mind.

I cried a lot, as I never cried before and never would again. Watching *Citizen Kane* on late-night TV, alone in the TV room, my parents in their bed, I thought I would not be able to stop, a kind of crying alien to me, as though I had been invaded. That little Rosebud sled. So many tears that in the end I had to believe it. That, and the urine test from the drugstore.

Becoming a mother, then, in a long tradition. Pregnancy first. Before the Pill, throughout history, half the mothers, half the marriages began this way. Almost all my friends were pregnant before they married. It was why they married. Although sometimes there were rumours or the familiar scent of scandal, the marriage was acceptable. The pending birth, a new baby was a reason to be glad.

Paré

But the leaving. The traditions of leaving being less traditional, less celebrated. The reasons less talked about or understood. Sadder.

There were no fine examples. No exemplars. No other mothers who had left their children in this particular way. That I knew. That I trusted. No other doctors' wives. No social workers. No family members. The only good mothers who left were mothers who had died. At least, that I knew. Things were changing, but not quite that fast. There were no self-help books listing the ten or twelve steps, describing possible pitfalls, telling readers how to avoid making the five predictable mistakes. No books I could give to my children or my parents or my parents-in-law that would tell them this was ordinary, more or less, that one in ten decent mothers leave their households this way. That it was, in fact, a positive predictor of resilience, agility, superior intelligence. That everything works out in the end. No call-in shows. No support groups. I was it. That I knew.

I was it and I was about to be gone. A fairytale mother. Gone. A fairytale within a fairytale. An old tradition. What happens to the gone mothers? Do they live inside their own fairytales?

The chop chop of the knife against the wooden board, squares of onion spinning and tears collecting in my eyes. As usual. This onion is yellow and fierce. I want to finish the job, scrape the bits into the pan, rinse the knife under cold water, clear my eyes. Then a sound bunts behind me. Not so much a sound as a sensation. Something at my back, breathing.

When I turn, nothing's there, although the air just above what I now think of as the burial place, that spongy dip in the kitchen floor near the sink that comes and goes — the air above it shimmers. And then a slightly accented voice says, You are making Suppe? A woman's voice, German maybe, but mellifluous as singing bowls.

My hands reek of onion. Ja, says the voice, rinse your hands. She must have heard me thinking. Don't worry, I won't leave, she says. Not that this worries me or that I'm asking her to stay. But I do what she says. I put the knife down and clasp my hands for a full minute under the force of cold water, then dry them on the towel under the sink.

See, she says, I'm still here.

No, I say to the empty space in front of me, I can't see you. I feel foolish, answering a disembodied voice, talking to nothing-really-there.

Of course, she says. Ja, sometimes I still forget. I am invisible in kitchens.

This strikes me as odd, because I'm always worrying about own invisibility, how much I can or can't be seen. If we go outside, to a park maybe, she says, you will see me. This occurs in kitchens. Ja, mainly now in kitchens.

What's going on? I say to myself, not wanting to address the voice again, give any more credibility to the shimmer that might be my imagination. I don't want to give in to some kind of west-coast airy-fairy weirdo stuff. So I test it, step forward — and whump right into a soft surface, a felted resistance. I stagger back. I've stepped on something. I back up, holding my hands out in front of me.

Okay then, let's go outside. I turn off the stove, grab my jacket from the chair, open the sliding glass door. Behind me, swishing and laboured breath. Despite her voice, this person must be old.

We tread the path to the carport, I can hear her in front — somehow she's gained on me — when suddenly I walk into an outstretched arm. Which is all I can see at first, hopping left to avoid it. One arm stuck out like a parking lot barrier. I wait stock still and watch her forming beside me. The one arm leads to her now-visible neck, and then her head, topped with a red taqiyah cap, round and flat-topped. Next her shoulders, upholstered red and glittering with tiny mirrors, swell below her neck. The rest of her materializes quickly, like a rabbit pulled from a top hat. The mirrors sparkle like miniature novas. Her feet appear in oxblood boots.

Beside me, human scale, an entire galaxy erupts and for a minute I hallucinate rainbows and auras, her shine becomes so intense. Bright rings festoon her fingers and her eyes are navy blue. I'm grateful that we both stand absolutely still. I'm inside a disco ball: any movement and I'd fall. I adjust my footing. She grips the handle of an old carpetbag covered with mirrors and embroidered figures. She's so short that the carpet bag drags on the grass. Her cheekbones look as heavy as two wooden spoons. She is steady as Cassiopeia, bright as the Polestar on a mid-winter night.

She touches my arm, and instinctively I pull my arm away, even though she's not big. She reaches out again, touches my shoulder, lightly. Tilts her head.

It's going to be alright, she says, straightening her mirrored back, creaking. At least as alright, she tips her chin, as these things can be. But you will need a companion. There's a lineage, a litany of us, you know, Cinderella's mother, Snow White's mother and Pinocchio's, the Little Match Girl's. Many others too. I am yours. Not your mother, of course. Your, you know, how you say, 'mentor.' Assigned by the rotation. Shall I leave this, she nods at her carpetbag, in the house, the spare room, perhaps?

I don't know what she means, the spare room, the carpetbag, leave it, or why or who she might be. Her dress is ancient and peculiar. I don't know what any of this can mean.

Why do I need a companion? Who are you? I don't need more complexity in my life. I don't know how or when or if I will be leaving. Through the sliding door. Not yet. I want to know why you're here with mirrors and your tattered carpetbag.

She reaches inside her voluminous skirts, draws out a small clay pipe, long-stemmed, white with a small brown bowl. She taps the bowl against her palm, releasing ash onto the grass, then puts the pipe between her lips and talks around it.

You are about to enter the other side of fairytale, she tells me, as if she knows how gravity works, as if she knows all about me. The side that looks like absence. It's not easy to reside through absence. Trials will naturally occur. Might you need a character witness. She laughs. Or counsel? There are always judgments, official and unofficial. She rearranges her face, serious now. Some occur entirely in our own minds.

I consider what she offers. I'm no stranger to judgment, I say, either side, judger and judged. I even judge myself.

Ja wohl, she nods. You see. Judgments, especially self-judgments, are hard to bear alone. You haven't left yet, but you will. There will be judgments. No one anticipates the quality or quantity of guilt. You need someone who understands.

I look at her as if she has two heads. Maybe she does. Maybe she carries the second one in her carpetbag. How does she know what she's talking about?

I've been around, she boasts. I know a lot. I read, sew, travel, knit. Ask me anything about the Dog Star. She tilts her face again. I can show you how to embroider with eighteen karat gold, how to stitch a cloud onto a hilltop in the evening.

How do you know I'll be leaving soon?

Experience. And the fairies. We fairytale gone-mothers keep up our connections. The fairies keep track of things. Part of their job description, ja? My job right now, at this very moment, is to be your guide as you go through this leaving now. This provokes a sloshing panic in my chest. I wish she'd stop saying leaving, absence. I feel invisible enough.

I'll stay awhile, she says, as if to reassure me. You're not the first. Fairytales teem with the absence of mothers, opening up room for big bad wolves and bloodied knives. Ja. My name is Gudrun, she curtseys. I live with others on the other side of town, the other side of the picket fence, which is to say, in another dimension. We support ourselves by various means.

By nefarious means?

Nein, various. You know, this and that. No government funding, no corporate sponsorship. Even if we wanted, we wouldn't qualify, ja? The unusual nature of our projects. Not your regular community group.

I feel I should be making a donation. We mend, she says, we make amends. Words and fabric, the fabric of the world. No one works with nettles anymore. Sometimes we play solitaire with little dogs. We take risks. Think of us as a collective. Collective consciousness. We tell stories. Good, bad, we all have stories. How else do we know our lives? How else does delight slide in, or guilt? My story, your story — I tell you, you tell me. We share. How else do we all mend?

I have a story I want to tell you, she looks me in the eye, which is my own story. There are people who live against the stream. My story runs against the stream. A distraction might be useful to you right now. She shrugs her shoulders. Whatever. You decide — I'm tired standing.

I glance at my watch — 1:38 p.m. Just me and the onions until the kids come home from school. A sudden gust whips her hat off, spinning like a Frisbee. I sprint after it, hand it back to her with a bow. Her hair is like spider webs about to blow away.

Let's have a cup of tea, I say to her. Who would not offer such an old woman tea and cookies? In the living room, I suggest.

I make us camomile. I need to calm down. Why not put your bag under the cot for now, I tell her, in the den, the spare room. Best if the kids don't see it, be no end of questions.

Gŭt, she says, as she lowers her weight into the armchair. Up close, her skin pleats like Ming Dynasty silk, faded and fine. She reaches inside a skin-pleat at her neck, tugs hard, removes one collar bone, then the other. Ahhh, she sighs. I feel as though I've been holding myself up by the scruff of my neck for days. She slides the bones into a pocket down the side of her skirt.

Were those your bones?

Who else would they belong to? She winks. At my age anything is possible. I've heard that Methuselah removed his ears in the early morning whenever the crows began their ragged saw. They say he shook out both his ears before he replaced them on his head — to remove unwanted sounds that had collected there. But he was older than I hope to be.

She sips her tea, still hot, then using the left side of her mouth she bites a cookie. I used to love these, she grins. Two teeth are missing and the rest are the colour of walnuts. Pfeffernüsse. I miss the red Suppe too, the way we made it in olden times. I was hoping you were making it when I saw you in the kitchen. So many things I still miss. Some things, she wings her hands, gone altogether. But the stories . . . one day you will tell yours.

Who would be interested in the story of an ordinary mother? I shake my head.

Another mother, of course. Which is to say, almost half the world. Are you interested in mine, Miene Lieblinge?

I am and I'm not. I have enough to think about. On the other hand, she seems determined. What can I say to her, this stranger who makes herself at home in my striped armchair? Another mother's story. Can it hurt? It would be a kindness. I feel her need for friendship. Mine too. Besides, I'm curious. So I say, go ahead. Until the boys get home.

Where are the children of the children? Waiting. The past is fading. Boundaries are fading and boundaries are forming. The table is set. The tablecloth, red. Blue bowls rest upon it. This morning presses on them. Where is the mother? Fading from the morning. Women are writing. With black in the middle. One bowl is cracked. With spoons at the sides. All this for the time when the children ascend the stairs. The cracks do not fade. Cereal boxes stand on the plastic cloth. The table is lit with half-sun. Half-cloud is on the table too. Half the cloth is lit with half the sun.

Over the Christmas holidays that year, the year before I left, before he knew anything about the changes that would be visited upon him, just before his tenth birthday, my youngest son turned to me one afternoon and snorted: *men*! As though he was the Wife of Bath or Anne Boleyn. Or me. I thought he was being funny, but he was serious; he was being an ally. I don't know which man, or men, had caused his disgruntlement at that particular moment. I don't know why he thought I needed an ally.

Back then, in the seventies and eighties, women were often furious with men, as a group, sometimes outraged and seething. Maybe some of it leaked into the children.

My youngest could have been a golf widow who, after telling her story of spousal neglect to a sympathetic neighbour over the backyard fence, finishes up with women's age-old summary complaint: *men*! As if there's nothing to do, nothing more to say. My youngest son bonding with his mother.

They used to say all women were just one husband away from welfare. All that winter when I thought about the possibility of leaving, I weighed my willingness to become a bag lady. I wasn't even certain I would qualify for welfare.

The social laws governing the mandatory creation of outsiders, like bag ladies, are as fixed as the natural laws that govern the speed of falling apples. The direction is as predictable, the drop as fast, the sudden contact with the ground as hard.

Bag ladies do not expect kindnesses. From anyone. Do not expect to be allowed. Into kitchens or bridge clubs or backyard swimming pools, into certain neighbourhoods, into families, into hearts. The social laws that legislate the inside and the out, who is and who is not allowed, the laws that regulate the in-and-out conditions are set to maintain the ordained balance. They keep those already out expecting nothing but slippery slopes, keep those already in alert for banana peels browning on the sidewalks of their ordered streets.

I had to steel myself. In case. I had to prepare myself. He had more money. He had more in, and more safe. In my mind, I was already out.

When he told his friends and his family, each one doled out their advice.

His boss said: Take her to a psychiatrist.

His mother said: If I were her, I'd roll over and go back to sleep.

His brother said: She's too feminine for this to happen.

His brother-in-law said: What will happen to the children?

When I told my friends and family, they doled out their advice.

My sister said: Marriage is not an endurance contest.

My married friend said: If you need money, let me know.

My unmarried friend said: The boys are older, they'll be fine without you to tuck them in at night.

My aunt said: Don't tell your father, it will kill him.

My mother said: Women are boring and fickle, but whatever you do, don't tell your father. If you do I'll take a gun and shoot you.

I knew my mother wouldn't take a gun and shoot me. Her heart was good, but she was a practical woman. She knew where the fun stopped and real life began. She was my mother after all: she knew everything would be blamed on her. She knew all mothers are to blame. It's the law.

⟿

Once upon a time, Gudrun cues her story, checks I'm listening, there was a mother and father and two children who lived in a cottage on the edge of the Black Forest.

I thought this was your own story? I say, confused by her use of the third person.

Ja, my own story, about my own self, she shakes her head. It is the way to tell my story. A Märchen. Like a fairytale, but not exactly.

I find it confusing. You're here in your first person, but you tell your own story in the third.

Okay, your way. I'll tell it first person, no italics.

The mother was Gudrun, me. The father, Heinrich, and the children, Hansel and Gretel. Ja, she says, this is a story about the fairytale Hansel and Gretel. But this is not that fairytale. This is the mother story.

More than five hundred years ago. She looks up for my reaction, but I don't let on, belief or disbelief. A stream looped behind our little cottage. Nothing remains, she sighs. Even the stream is buried. Cars on the Autobahn from Frankfurt to Würzburg zoom directly over where it used to be. But five hundred years ago, sparrows ate breadcrumbs from our palms. Hansel and Gretel loved the little bird feet gripping round their fingers. We lived in the forest and filled our days with firewood and bread, games with white pebbles, games with string, imitating sparrow song. We were young; it would not last.

Not that it was heaven. Nein, nein! In the forest wolves howled at night, their eyes firing the darkness, they ate anything that moved after the sun had bloodied up the western sky. In the morning, you have no idea! We found the empty boots of those who'd wandered too far at night, boots empty except for ruddy stumps. Foxes waited after dark beyond the chicken coop to eat our chickens and our cats. Ghosts too, who captured children to suck the marrow from their finger bones. But for all that, it was almost heaven. By day. She taps her left boot — my knife-blade, she grins. Even small children carried knives in their boots or strapped to belts.

A sound like hooves at my kitchen door: my boys galloping up the back stairs, racing each other into the kitchen, shoving, red-faced, panting, shouting, Mum Mum, ya gotta see… But they jerk to a stop once inside, suddenly quiet, turning their heads left and right, sensing something. Then they drop their books and bags on the kitchen table. One makes for the fridge, the other for the basement stairs.

That Saturday in June, the zipper strained on my suitcase, which hunched by the kitchen door. I finished my toast and peanut butter. He had arrived home from his girlfriend's place with his girlfriend, my replacement. He stood at the kitchen sink washing dishes, waiting for the kettle to boil to make tea for her, while she read in the backyard. We had nothing much to say. Kettle boiling. The space of a thousand psychic miles, nothing to say between us for the long ten months just passed when we walked from fridge to sink, from sink to stove, scratching our soft soles on shards of shell. We hardly dared to raise our eyes. Afraid to catch each other. Who would we see? What would we say? For months all small-talk mined with eggshells.

In April, three months before I left, he cried. Collapsing on the grey velvet sofa, he smashed his face into the cushions and cried as if he'd never stop. I don't remember if I'd ever seen him cry before.

After we closed the front door, having just farewelled our dinner guests, doctors and doctors' wives, he turned to me and said, Isn't Sam's wife beautiful. We carried on our social lives that year as if we led an ordinary married life together, as if nothing had changed between us. Most friends didn't know. We threw dinner parties and sent Christmas cards. We attended events together. A facade. We didn't know how else to conduct our family life, which was shattering in slow motion.

Yeah, she's gorgeous. I said it like a dyke. I don't know why, maybe to show him who I was now, maybe to make things more real, maybe to retaliate because it still hurt when he said another woman was beautiful. Maybe because she was beautiful. It caught him off guard and he choked suddenly on an intake of ordinary hallway air, starting to sob under the harsh hall light, his face dissolving. He stumbled into the living room like he'd just then realized. He buried his face in the velvet cushions, his body stretched six feet along the sofa's length, taking up the whole sofa and then some.

I perched on the sofa-arm beside his feet, which flopped over the end, his shoes still on, and I watched his body shiver and convulse. So loud, I thought he'd wake the kids. I wanted to stroke his head or rub his back, but I thought, I'm not the one to comfort him any longer. Now that I was his source of sadness, my comfort wasn't any comfort. But I stayed with him, close to his feet, one hand on the heel of one of his plain brown shoes, and waited for the rip-tide to finish with him. He's a big man; it took a long time.

We lived in Montreal until the boys were seven and nine. Before we moved to Vancouver, we spent summers and weekends at a cottage in the Laurentians, an extended family complex, several cottages on a lake, with family all around, his parents, his aunts and uncles, nieces, nephews, brothers- and sisters-in-law, cousins, his grandmother.

Driving north on the Laurentian Auto Route, on Friday nights, both boys fast asleep, their heads pillowed in my lap in the back seat of our new gold-coloured Datsun. Long before car seats or seat belts. We risked all our lives every time we drove the car.

I studied their sleeping profiles, their plump cheeks at rest. I memorized the infinities of their ears, which I would gentle with the tip of my baby finger, careful not to wake them, brushing the soft furls and swirls, as though I was a collector, cleaning, counting up the facets of their innocence.

The year we lived in Nairobi we were alone. I was twenty-five, they were babies. No family. No old friends. Bougainvillea climbed the walls and wrought-iron railings of the apartment building on Protectorate Road, on the edge of downtown. Red, purple, orange, pink and white, the bougainvillea bloomed like bunting, ribbons and bows. Every day the scent of eucalyptus wafted through the barred and open windows. Sunshine bright as Klieg lights every day till six. Then sudden night. Like a curtain falling: no long sunsets, no evenings until bed. Just day. Then night.

In October the rains came in the afternoons, rivering from the sky. Gutters, roads, fields drowning. The jacaranda bloomed that month, the cool purple-blue haunting branches still bereft of leaves.

When he left us in the morning, driving to the Kenyatta General in the middle of the city, they climbed into bed with me, snuggling close, filling up the depression he had left in the mattress. I held them and they held me. We were each others' companions, all day, sometimes into night. They were my reason and my solace. We were far from home, it took months and months for us to find other things to hold that year.

Don't watch (I want to warn) through the kitchen door. Avert your boyish eyes. The door, the way it slides, don't listen, the way it rumbles in the groove. Don't. Watch me. My suitcase. The colour of tobacco. My uncertain grip. Filled with three days' worth of underwear. The way I step across. And out. As if I knew. The line between the in and out.

Don't. Watch. Me cross. (I want to shield their eyes.) Into another life. Don't wave me down the wooden steps. Don't throw smooches or confetti, rotten shoes or over-ripe tomatoes. Don't watch me turn the key, back the Aspen wagon from the carport, silver as a bullet, down the lane, past the Murrays and the Chans. Leaving. Past the little dog that always barks behind its backyard fence. Past the stop sign on the corner.

Don't. A mother's word, a small attempt to keep the children safe. Don't run. Don't touch. Don't look. Don't cry.

Three days from now. Me, back up the wooden steps. The sliding door. Don't listen to the grumble in the groove. Don't watch the way I step back into in as if I had not been gone. My uncertain grip. As if I still belonged. Nothing changed. The clock. The kitchen. Three days gone. The colour of tobacco. Don't.

I will pour whole milk into glasses with pirates painted on the side. I will stir the soup. Lean against the counter. Listen.
                    As if nothing. As if I never …

⤚

Once a week was market day, says Gudrun. I collected eggs and herbs and stacked everything into the wooden cart, which the children and I pulled to the village where we sold what we could to villagers. One day Hansel and Gretel woke up with stomachs round as poisoned pups, having eaten golden berries which appeared that summer on the far side of the creek. So I went to market without them. I left bread and healing brews. Keep the door locked, I told them, don't answer it. I'll be back at dark. Your father will be back tomorrow night.

At the end of the day, a dwarf in red velvet appeared. My name is Tomas, he said, bowing. One of his eyes wandered in its socket, it was hard to meet his gaze. I come with an urgent request, he continued, to heal my friend, Astrid, who has been cursed. I did not hesitate despite my worry about the children; I am a healer. I stuffed my herbs into my pockets and left the cart with the old woman who lived beside the market.

I lean in, excited, thinking the action is about to start. But Gudrun closes her eyes, falls asleep and disappears.

Paré

Gudrun appears again a week later, giving no reason for her absence, and I don't ask. I question nothing of her comings and goings. With her, I live in an altered universe or state. I make tea, set out cookies. She sucks on the stem of her clay pipe.

Tomas and I arrived at a camp encircled with caravans. All colours. Across the camp's opening a bearded man led a black bear, which without warning, leapt its leash in my direction. The man grabbed his collar and with a mighty tug, pulled him away. I thought it remarkable, not so much that the bear lunged — bears are known to be unpredictable — but that the man was so strong that the bear whimpered as he was led away.

We entered Astrid's caravan at the far end of the camp. She lay on a cot, wearing a shift with a bib of beadwork. Her hair was matted, wild as a lion's mane around her face. Her hands were clawed.

How long? I asked her.

Tomas answered: three days.

Who did this? I asked her, again. She growled, as if in answer, but she could not form words.

Tomas answered. Père Fraq, he said, the man with the bear. He's done this before, though never yet on one of our own troupe. His animals are under this sort of spell. Drunken villagers maybe, or performers from other troupes perhaps, but not one of us. His animals once were humans too, he said, and lowered his head.

I asked Tomas to return to my village to tell the old woman to send word to my children that I would not be home that night. Tomas left the caravan, his steps receding down the short set of stairs and across the camp. I touched Astrid's head and chanted words I'd heard my mother chant. I spit into Astrid's palms and rubbed her hands together. I fed her bitter teas. Sie nähte alle Nacht.

Finally I collapsed beside her. For seven days and seven nights we slept, as if under a spell. Maybe we were; those old days were filled with every kind of spell. We woke on the morning of the eighth day to sunshine swording through chinks in the walls and Astrid's fur clumped on the caravan floor. Astrid's own shining hair surrounded her face and she said, Fräulein, smiling at me, the softest voice I have ever heard, and my heart opened to her like the wings of a raven. Such a miracle, Astrid said to me, you must be an angel. And I thought the same of her.

She was not yet twenty. Fierce though. I was not yet twenty-five. And I knew, you see, right away, as soon as she named me her angel. I don't know why. We were young. I had seen women in their beds before, in pain, giving birth. But her eyes. Her cheeks, ripe peaches. Her spirit, the way she healed, the way she regarded me. I was besotted. I miss her to this day.

Have you had enough fairytale, enough enchantment for today? she asks me.

I shake my head. It's only just beginning — carry on until the boys come home. So she does, briefly. Her eyes are wet.

While we slept those days and nights, the caravans, and our caravan with them, rolled on farther and farther east. When we woke, we were leagues away. I had expected to get an early start home, taking Astrid with me to keep her safe from Fraq. But life was now more difficult. Tomas never did return to the troupe, nor would he have been able to. The caravans had travelled too far, even that first night. We never saw Tomas again.

Apologia for My Oldest Son

When he was four years old I dreamt he was run over by a jeep.   In Africa.   He was walking on the sand a distance behind me; and when I turned, the jeep was bearing down.   I couldn't save him.   He was too far away.   The jeep backed up and drove over him a second time.   I ran over the impossible sand.   It took forever.   When I picked him up, he turned into a bird.   Maybe he was a dove.   I folded him, still hurt, into my shirt, thinking: *I need to take him home.*   It didn't trouble me that he was now a bird.

I have never told him how he still seems winged to me.   He has a faith that he will survive.   He has a way that allows him to be kind.   And a patience for the way life is. He is kind to almost everyone, including me, who one night when he was only four, killed him under the wheels of a jeep, though he then became a dove, signalling his beneficence, the way he would endure.

In 1970, two years before we moved to Nairobi, I joined a CR group. Two babies under three and snowbound winters that stretched all the way through May. A few months after I proposed that he and I should both work part-time so we could be equal. Which he declined, replying, not until you can earn as much as me. Which was reasonable in its own way, given our finances. But not democratic.

Before I left for the CR meeting that first night, I stood at the mirror and wriggled into my Army and Navy sweater, the coarse blue wool so tight that I had to adjust my breathing. That Army and Navy sweater meant business. I sucked in my tummy and zipped up my jeans.

Where are you going? he asked me from the bedroom door.

Susan's place, with your sister. A CR group, I added, almost an after-thought.

CR?

Yeah, consciousness raising, you know, Women's Liberation. Like Mao did in the Chinese Revolution.

The doorbell rang. The kids were in bed. His sister stamped her feet in our vestibule. We were already late. She hugged her brother hello. Cold, she warned me, wear your parka.

CR? he said to her.

Oh yeah, she smiled, women only; going to be revolutionary.

Back later, I yelled as I closed the door.

CR was how we saved our lives, twelve women meeting every month for almost two years. Telling our stories and our complaints to each other. Refusing to shave our legs or underarms or wear lipstick or bras. Talking: why, how, what we should do about how women were not allowed to be equal. About how bras cut off our breath. We threw them away along with the eye liner. More comfortable that way. Thursday nights, we could not stop talking. All the things wrong with the world. Questioning everything: high heels, girdles, the nuclear family, monogamy, why men earned more money, why men couldn't do the dishes, why women couldn't be CEOs, why the waiter always asked the man to taste the wine. We read radical texts and radical poetry. Women's Liberation became the Women's Movement became Feminism became the Second Wave. We met in each other's kitchens. We said: Why can't they stay home with the kids? We said: Why can't we run the world? For eighteen months those meetings opened up the sky. The half that we held up. We would never be the same. We were furious, exhilarated. On the edge of the world, the world spinning faster, spinning whole cloth way out on the margins.

Two CR members became lesbians that first year. Together. Which made sense to me. But it also seemed odd, as if they had turned into meadowlarks or marsh hawks overnight. One of them left the group. The other stayed, but we didn't really know how to talk to her anymore. What do you say to a meadowlark?

One night after a CR meeting, my sister-in-law and I stomped Montreal's frozen streets, warming our feet and then stopping, after quick shoulder-checks, to paste feminist stickers on the brick wall of the Playboy Club on Aylmer Street, on a sports car parked outside the club, on the door of a bank down the street. I don't remember where we got the stickers. They said: *This Hurts Women.* The owner of the Porsche scurried towards us as we plastered the sticker on the windscreen of his car. He yelled, hey, you can't do that. But we could. And we did.

Some days I want to sink into that soft burial place underneath the kitchen floor, into the sink-hole, down with all the bones accumulating, the broken shoes, crumpled shirts, the used-up words, the spongy tennis balls. Pull a blanket over my head, rest inside where I used to be, with them, and with the me who used to be.

Once, those bones resided inside their rightful skin, ordinary bones in ordinary constellations, now a sort of midden, no knowing whose bones are whose. A skull filled up with chicken bones nests inside the bones of an open hand. A fibula supports a collar bone, a necklace. No knowing whose bones dovetail whose pain. Where one pain ends, another overlaps, like feathers, pinated on a wing. Words on words rustling in a skull.

Where to find the one who left, the one who made the hard decision not to stay, not to tuck her children into bed at the end of every day. Hard to believe now that she was really there, deciding.

Why did she believe in fit, not fit? Why did she believe that if she fit into one, she could not fit into the other? Mother, lesbian. Whatever the answer, it was a belief of long standing.

Whatever the answer, no one else was fit enough to tuck her children in at the end of every day.

Paré

Always at night the universe blacked out; it caused
tremendous fear.   Children knew to trust only the day.

The word mother is at once too large and too small.
Who can keep up with such a word, especially in the dark?

In 2001, scientists discovered the universe was turquoise,
even at night.   After countless millennia — such relief.

Later that year, citing flaws in the original study, scientists reported
the universe was beige.   The sales of Prozac soared.

These colours are just colours, but they affect our minds,
reflect how lost we are.   No mother can be present

at all times.   All children play under false pretences,
blue sky is only one of them.

My mother preferred the colour beige. Personally, I think it's only suitable for carpeting in certain public buildings. My mother longed to wear beige sweaters and beige raincoats, but she worried that beige drained the colour from her face. She wore it often enough. A fawn-coloured skirt, a sand-coloured blouse. It would have pleased her to know the universe was in fact beige.

In her coffin, she wore a dress the colour of weathered wood or sparrow wings or pebbles under water, the colour of reluctance, not wanting to leave, not wanting to be left.

Paré

I told my mother that I was a lesbian. We were driving past Kitsilano Beach. She had come to visit from Ottawa and the Vancouver day filled with seagulls and blue sky. That was when she said that women were boring. And fickle.

We are? I said. I think it scared her to think of me as different from her. As though I was now on another team. I think it scared her to think of the undoing that was about to happen. Three years later she was dead.

My mother's sister, my aunt, told me I caused my mother's cancer. By becoming a lesbian.

Apologia for My Youngest Son

Let these words fall around him, the way snow or petals, at his feet, might fill his new Italian shoes, the pockets of his jacket, the hem of his corduroy pants, the ones he wears to work, where he takes a call from a teacher reporting a boy is standing on the roof of the school. The boy's eleven and this morning he had a fight with his mother. And my son puts on his jacket and drives to the school and by the time he arrives, the boy, only eleven, just turned, sits in the principal's office, his face a tight bud. He stares out the window and my son makes arrangements for him and his mother. They will come to his office and talk to him and tell him secrets no one else knows. Let my words too, tell him what no one else knows, making no sound, or maybe sounding like snow or petals of stargazer lilies when they leave the stem. They leave a stain.

Snow falls apart as it falls away. Words too. I carry these with me, afraid to fell them at his feet. But where else. Tell me: has an armful of petals ever caused harm? Or an armful of snow, too much cold? My son never stood on the roof of a school, but some days now I think of him at ten or maybe eleven, just turned. The strength it took. Which is what these words would say, if I could. Like flowers. Onto his shoulders. Into the palms of his hands, into his careful ears hearing the story of the mother and the boy who came down from the roof. Another story. Let this story, these petals, fall into his hair, my son's hair, onto the collar of his shirt, landing soundlessly, stopping in the pocket that covers his heart.

That day, leaving. A bed, a dresser and a chair occupied the room I was moving to in a friend's house fifteen blocks away, so I didn't have to move furniture from my own house. But I needed a lamp. I propped the lamp in the back of the station wagon, wedged it between my suitcase and a box of towels and sheets. Put the lampshade on top of the box.

Later I installed a small bookcase from home, and a grey and white poster of an unmade bed. In 1980, that particular art poster, a black and white photograph of a rumpled bed, was ubiquitous.

I didn't want to take too much from the kids' house; they still had to live there like it was the same house as before. Same house, only every other week, their mother wasn't in it. I was already taking enough away.

They rushed into the kitchen when I called them that Saturday in June, the day I was leaving. He stood at the counter drying the teapot. When I called their names my throat emptied, like their names were leaving me, like I was letting their names go from me. But I said them anyway. They raced into the kitchen, stumbling and sweaty with their homemade haircuts, hair flopping around their faces like live silk, their striped rugby shirts, green and white, blue and yellow, their cheeks hot from running and the heaviness of the day. I had to look away.

Let's all sit down at the table, I said. I was already seated. I could hardly breathe.

But Davey is waiting for us out front. They shuffled their feet.

This is important. It won't take long, I said. My older son looked at his brother, who pulled out a chair, scraping it over the linoleum. Their faces fell serious, just like ours.

Your mother wants to tell you something, their father said as he took his seat at the end of the table.

I didn't actually want to, but I said, You know how things have been a little unsettled this winter. They widened their eyes, looking from me to their father.

We have a plan now. They looked back at me. You are going to stay living here in this house and your dad and I will take turns living here with you. I'm going to leave today — in a little while. But I'll be back on Monday, in just two days, and then I'll stay for a week. After that your dad will come back and stay with you for the next week. You'll stay living in this house. As though I was reading out the rules to a new board game. Things will be the same for you. Dad and I will go back and forth. We'll see how it goes. The shock of it lit up their eyes. They couldn't even look at each other.

We'll have family meetings. No one else said anything; their father's mouth set in a bowed line above his chin. Not much will change for you, not really. I wanted it to be like that: nothing much changed.

But then a storm swirled over the table, out of nowhere it jelled the air, sheet-lightning pulsed overhead. I braced for rolling thunder; their boy-faces filling up with thunder. I thought: please don't let them ask me who will tuck them in at night. I don't know, I don't know anything anymore. Maybe this would have been their question — who will tuck us in — maybe they had other questions, other things to say or yell. But they were children. They didn't say anything. The thunder was deafening: it flung itself against the walls.

I'd come this far, made myself believe they were old enough, that it would be alright, but I didn't know. I'd started things; now things were moving on their own. Gale force.

No one cried that morning, sitting still and staring. No one said I'm sorry, no one yelled, no one smashed the table with a fist, no one hit out, no one called a lawyer, no one called the grandparents, nobody swore or cursed, nobody threw a vase or a rolling pin, nobody threw a fit, nobody ran to the knife drawer, no one stomped to their room, nobody slammed a door, no one plugged their fingers in their ears, no one said how dare you, no one screamed, no one said how sad.

Only the table between us. The clock over the fridge.

Finally they said, Can we go now and play with Davey? Their eyes studying the oilcloth.

Yes, I said, but come back in twenty minutes, before I have to go. Already I had less right to ask, but I asked them anyway, to come back so I could kiss them good-bye, hold them in that kitchen, that was our kitchen, before I opened the sliding door and walked away.

They were ten and nearly twelve the day I left. When I left again, in a full-time way, they were thirteen and nearly fifteen. Now they are forty-one and nearly forty-three.

I say I never really left them. Though they were left without me. Sometimes.

I am always trying to finish the job. They tell me: It's already finished.
My youngest says: In my life, in my job, I save children.
My oldest says: In my life, in my family, I cradle my sons.

How does a mother leave? How does she direct her feet? She must tell herself stories that may or may not be true. She must tell herself whatever it takes to make it possible to leave. She must tell herself her children are old enough. They do not need her anymore. That she has nothing more to offer. That her husband is a kind father. That she will be there when they call her on the phone. She must tell herself there is no other answer. That they need their father more, their friends more, their school more. That she doesn't want a battle. For the children's sake. That she will make it work. Make believe.

That is the first step. A lot depends on what she reads and who is there to talk to. A lot depends what year it is, what season, what weather, what time of day, or if a wishbone lies drying on the sill.

How does a mother understand her leaving years ago? The future looking back. How does she recognize herself, accept that she took the steps away? How does she accept her younger steps walking from past into the future of someone she isn't yet? Would she recognize herself in a police line-up?

I was looking for happiness, you know, like the Buddha was looking for happiness when he left his wife, his newborn baby. And you might say: isn't everyone? Looking for happiness.

The kind of happiness I was looking for I wasn't going to find where I was living. It wasn't simple sex or companionship, it was justice too, it was a more meaningful meaning. It was changing the world, more elbow room for women.

Like the Buddha. Only a little different. Maybe I give myself airs. But that was how it was.

And I found it. Some happiness. Some meaning. Elbow room.
I found some sadness too.

94

If you brush carefully, if you look closely at their bones from that day you will see that they are the bones of young children, only ten and eleven, almost twelve, fine and growing bones, slender, almost flexible.

If you look at the bones of their parents you will see that these bones are the bones of young adults, only thirty-two and thirty-five, fully grown, but not the bones of elders, accustomed to making impossible decisions. These were the people, all young, making those decisions. All the elders lived in other cities and none of them had been through this kind of thing. No one to suggest the purchase of a duplex. In all the generations before, no one had ever dealt with this sort of thing before.

The table is lit with half-sun.   Half-cloud is on the table too.   Half the cloth is lit with half the sun.   With spoons upon it.   Stainless steel half-fills with glint.   The minutes fade.   The time.   The morning.   Presses down.   Where is the guilt?   At the side. With white light in the bowls of the spoons.   The house is fading.

Did I mention Sappho, Gudrun asks, snipping a thread from a cloth draped over her lap. She has grown very at home in my home when no one else is home.

Sappho?

Ja, the poet. She's in our group. Classy member, early, maybe even founding. Good with words.

But your group is for mothers, fairytale mothers. She doesn't fit the profile.

Fit, schmit, says Gudrun. She fits! We make room. Virgin Mary too. Not so exclusive. In the fairytale of literature, Sappho is the mother of lyric poetry, same as Homer is father of epic — ja? She is mother! Well-known too, but in fragments only. Plenty of absence. The Virgin Mary too, assumpted up. Gone. But I'm trying to become less absent, you know, more visible in kitchens.

Why? I ask.

So Hansel and Gretel can find me where they knew me best. Her eyes go all dreamy. I practise, she says. Finger by finger, more and more visible.

Want a ham sandwich? Trying to shift the mood that has settled between us. She often becomes gloomy when she mentions her children.

You have Black Forest?

Turns out I do. And two Kaiser rolls in the bread box.

When I bring her the sandwiches, Gudrun is humming a Lieder tune. Her left foot is missing.

See, she points, I can hide my foot. This is good. Control. Sometimes I hide, sometimes I show. My decision. While munching on her Kaiser, she squeezes her eyes shut and her foot returns. I did that, she slaps her knee, laughs, ham sandwich still in her mouth. Then she continues with her story.

Ah yes. Falling in love with Astrid, sure. Hearts big as the Alps. Old story, ja. But waking to the shock that the caravans have travelled too far. The middle of panic, but also exhilaration, in love. Lost and lost. It doesn't take much. The freedom made me dizzy for days.

Astrid recovered, fur moulted, teeth shrank. But she could not perform that night when we stopped in a village near Salzburg. And then, just before the show began, Fraq swung open our caravan door, glaring at me, cursing me for interfering with his spell. He was bold. You shall never see your children alive again, he growled at me. They shall wither away at the sight of you. He spat on my foot. Then he slammed the door. Who could bear this? True, I am a healer, I know spells, but who could take the chance. Spells are spells, but unspellings are always uncertain.

We leave immediately, I told Astrid.

But this is where I live, I have no other home, she replied.

And become a performing animal? I reminded her.

Gudrun picked at the bag of fabric in her lap. Enough for now, she said.

At 10:55 p.m. he opened the door, flicked on the overhead light, looked around our bachelor apartment on Durocher Street and started, Why didn't you clean up the dinner dishes, put away the ketchup maybe. The butter, at the very least. We'd been married five months, living in an apartment so small our queen-size wedding present bed crowded most of what was supposed to be the living room. The kitchen, a one-person galley, smelled of fried onions and that night dirty dishes covered all the counter space.

Too tired, I yawned. Turn off that overhead.

But you had all evening while I was at the hospital. He didn't add, *saving lives*, he didn't need to, it was always understood.

I am very pregnant, in case you haven't noticed. It makes me very tired. And at 8:45 tomorrow morning I will stand in front of thirty-five grade four boys and teach them long division. Half of whom do not speak English yet. I did not get out of bed.

He was mad that night. Maybe saving lives that shift had been more distressing than usual. I was exhausted. It was late spring and every day my basketball of a stomach expanded another inch underneath my tent dress. I had only four dresses. My mother had made three of them. He started banging around the semi-kitchen trying to clean up. Then I got mad too; my perpetual heartburn flared. It was our first fight, even though I was too tired, even though he was too tired too, out half the night, saving lives.

I rolled out of bed. We cleaned up the kitchen together, still fighting under our breaths. In all our thirteen years together, we only had a handful.

Paré

first fight: dishes
        he said: why didn't you
        she said: why don't you
        he said: but you were home
        she said: but you're home now

second fight: Risk
        he said: I win
        she said: I won last night
        she said: I'll win tomorrow night
        he said: I'll win tomorrow,
        I'll win the night after tomorrow night

third fight: wishes
        she said: I want a job
        he said: when you can earn as much as me
        she said: both work half-time
        he said: you'll never earn as much as me

fourth fight: vicious
        he said: something about lunch
        she said: something else about lunch
        she threw: a box of Kleenex at him
        he threw: a knife into the floor
        (or was it the other way around)

fifth fight: wallpaper
        he said: nothing
        he climbed down the ladder
        she said: what?
        he walked out the door
        she made the dinner

last fight: politics
        he said: what did I do?
        she said: you were not a woman;
        not so much do, as be
        he said: what?
        she said: nothing

Paré

The bones of my mother buckle my feet,
tap dance the kitchen floor.
My milk-teeth broke my tender gums.

My children pressed their eyelids
against my not being there.   They
roam the site between the stove

and the kitchen sink, where half
my days I'd stood, trying to avoid
the upward seep of damp.

I blame my father's mandible.   I blame
the metacarpals of my mother's hands.
My children will blame

my bones, the cage that held
their foetal hearts.   They will grow suspicious
of their baby teeth, the falsity of expectation.

We climbed the carpeted staircase, dim lit, to the Hawaiian Lounge on St. Catherine Street to watch a drag show. Impersonations of Judy Garland and Carol Channing. A double date that night, a year after our first babies were born. An odd choice for entertainment, I thought, but cool. It was the other couple's idea. They were our best friends. I guess it beat playing another game of Password in their living room, the usual way to spend a Friday night with our babies asleep in the bedroom across the hall. I guess we all had enough money for a babysitter that night.

At the end of Carol Channing's "Diamonds Are a Girl's Best Friend," I left the table to find the women's washroom. In my A-line skirt and V-neck sweater, I felt a little out of place, coiling through the tables, watching for the women's sign, traversing the lounge in front of all those homosexual eyes. In another dimension altogether, pretending I belonged.

A few women slouched against the bathroom walls, or leaned, one leg over a stool, smoking, growling at each other, their snarling exchanges bouncing off the black and white honeycomb tiles. One woman, louder than the others, shouted to a woman inside one of the stalls, I'll kill you if I ever catch you, so help me, I'll take a knife, you think I won't, her lower lip balancing a Gitan. B'en shit I will.

The bathroom attendant, an older woman in a light blue shift, checked me out from her perch near the entrance. I had entered another country. It had little to do with me except that I needed to pee. But it was more exciting than the drag show, which wasn't unexciting.

Strangely, I thought even at the time, those bathroom women didn't scare me with their growls and knives. I did not feel unsafe. If they had been men snarling like that I might have felt scared. Only men scared me. Only some of them.

—⁊

That night we left, slinking out of camp before the sun rose. Astrid talked about Fraq as we walked forest paths. A defrocked priest, she said, who joined the troupe, striding into our camp one winter day, leading a line of tethered beasts, a white horse, a giant bear, five Russian wolves, muzzled, and seven French poodles, each one red. The troupe was struggling that year, she said, three performers had died of the pestilence, and when he entered the camp, we were as hungry as we had ever been. They welcomed him.

Those animals could perform such tricks, Astrid told me. Whatever Fraq commanded. The bear danced, of course, but also swallowed fire. It would genuflect, lumbering onto one knee whenever friars were in the audience, causing villagers great glee. The wolves sang Russian folk tunes, and not too badly and the poodles spoke French, of course, but English too. The horse played chess, nudging pawns and bishops across the board with its muzzle. The horse often won, but never against Fraq. Fraq had only to nod his head and his animals would do anything. They never lost their human eyes — the way human eyes grow wide with fear.

Astrid had nightmares as we travelled. Her screams endangered us. My own dreams were of my children. We woke from agony into fear, but we woke in each other's arms. On the twelfth night the rains began. From then on, we travelled in mud.

In the middle of our third week of travel, I woke up to the sound of growling in Astrid's throat. I could smell him before I could see anything at all. The smell of his bear. Fraq stood over me, grabbing for my throat. His meaty breath too close.

I was warned never to utter these words, so I said them quickly, in another language altogether. Ending with the curse, may you die. Fraq lept away. He understood. His last words to me were, may you live.

Gudrun pats her chest — she's still alive. She folds her hands in her lap, sighs. Which curse is worse? she asks me. How would I know?

everything at risk   everything at peace   no seat belts   no car seats   limitless   quiet as night's eye despite this Friday night engine hum   this eight-lane-highway-heading-north   this innerspace   three of us between the backseat doors   their baby heads lapped on my denim knees   their father at the wheel upfront   this time of night   this almost speed-of-fairy-light   I close my eyes   heading for Cassiopeia   beyond the farthest rings of Saturn   this faith in immortality   these days of the universe expanding lights along the highway ticking off the effervescent miles   sloughing off the everyday the faint green glow of dashboard haze   slipping domestic bonds of gravity   this ordinary round of life   we change the known world   wear peace between our fingers   purple beads around our necks   one baby cheek the full-pink moon   one ear shines forty-karat gold   lunar moths protect their cocooned eyes   I worship at their profiles in this sacred backseat space   this Datsun mothership homing through the silky threads   the Milky Way   these endless galaxies   darkness domed   our hopeful consequential hearts   everything completely safe   or not at all

~∂

For weeks we travelled in circles, unable to find our way. So when we came upon performers folding up their tents, we joined them. We wanted something more than toadstools and minnows. We had no map. We were exhausted. I doubted everything.

The Famous Magyar Performing Troupe of Great and Wondrous Spectacles boasted a fire-eater, a knife-thrower, a juggler, a fortune-teller, five musicians, dancers, a bear, a wild cat, clowns, acrobats, a magician, a bearded lady, but no aerialist — until we arrived. And I could stitch their costumes and their knife wounds, heal boils and runny noses. We travelled with that troupe for a long time, to the farthest reaches of Christendom. At the end of every day, I prayed for my children, that one day I would see them. In those days I still prayed.

Months later, we learned that Fraq had died. An old dishevelled friar told us one day. He'd heard it from a pedlar. Fraq drowned while fishing in a swollen river. The rains, endless that year, filled fields to overflowing, wagon wheels to their axles, lowlands stood in fetid pools. Fraq drowned in a reckless, rocky river, an ancient carp pulling harder on the line than he, and his pockets filled with silver. An animal trainer, yes, but, not of fish. Always loopholes. And of course, my curse.

In the kitchen the oven-timer pings. I check the cookies. When I return to the living room, Gudrun is gone. I call, check the spare room, but she's disappeared. She does that sometimes, vacates the space around her, whether by her own volition or not is hard for me to tell, though she usually stays for cookies.

Where do the real-gone mothers go? Are they living on the other side of town, east of the picket fence, across the tracks, where they smoke Player's Light on sagging stoops and cough all night? Do they play solitaire with little dogs? Do they shop for overcoats at St. Vincent de Paul, buy bashed-in tins of tuna? Case lots of mushroom soup?

Do they wear black shawls, confess their absences to priests? Are they really gone? Do they ask blackbirds the whereabouts of Hansel? Do they pray, their real-gone lives filling up with crows and flaked tuna, unbearable news? Do the crows, breadcrumbs in their beaks, always tell the truth?

Can the mothers stop themselves from weeping if only if only they'd been there to save the children from the cinders and the gingerbread, from queens with mirror mirrors on the wall. Their hands raised in supplication: Who tucks them in at the day's end?

So many doors into and out of this story.   One door leads to the carport.   One door leads out of the bedroom.   Two doors for the kitchen with shards of shell and tea-spoons bent in two.   How many steps to wear out the decision?   Thinned between the breast bone and the spine, wear, tear, the break where everything collects, spilled milk and broken eggs, Cheerios.   The site you try to wipe away, the place where every kitchen stores its mess.   The bottom of the bowl.

It is just time.   Just broken bones.   One door to the basement.   Once a little dog with a blue and silver collar.   A window through which a wren, where finches in a tree, an old black crow.   The way the wind whips round a room.   Doors slam, slide, pinch a finger, catch a foot.   Panes of glass fill up with past.   Walls concave with rain, the sluice of time.   Through the open door, the threat of evening as the sun absents the sky.

During our first year together in our second small apartment, a flat in a nineteenth-century house on St. Famille, we started playing Risk, a board game that pits players' armies against each other. The armies, represented by tiny candy-coloured plastic cubes: blueberry, lime, orange, cherry, lemon, or liquorice. Both of us always grabbed for the liquorice pieces, based on the traditional understanding that black was pretty much the only winning colour for an army. What kind of victory could cherry cubes ever hope to exact? We played every night he wasn't at the hospital, setting up the board after dinner, after our baby was asleep in his crib.

With his new Minolta, he snapped a picture of me one night, the board lying on the brown sofa beside me. I had lost the game. Maybe I'm crying, maybe I'm screaming: my hair covers my face and my hands are in the air. We each had winning streaks and losing streaks. He snapped that picture during one of my longer losing streaks. No, I shouted at him, my hands flailing to hide my face, like someone being taken away in a police car. Don't you dare. But he snapped it anyway. He wanted to record my hard luck. I never did get a shot of him in one of his losing streaks; the camera belonged to him.

His sister joined us for dinner one night that winter, and after dinner, right after the baby fell asleep, we set up the board in the living room. For three. We may have let her use the black pieces. But maybe not. When the game was over she advised us to stop playing Risk. Forever. Put the game away and never bring it out again. She looked at us sternly. That game brings out the worst in both of you.

When we weren't playing Risk, we worked as a team, agreeing on the basics about almost everything. People thought we had an ideal marriage. From the outside looking in, except for Risk, we looked pretty good. That year when the summer arrived, we took his sister's advice and gave the game away, like addicts who had bottomed out, who had finally seen the light.

My far-away ears, my reckless not-knowing. If peace enters it will be drenched with rain, soaked with night. I thought they were old enough. They had their father, each other. They had pet cats and their friends. That these would be sufficient. Their street safe with houses in a row, hedges, lawn mowers, cars in driveways, milk in waxed cartons, BMX bikes, baseball gloves and Hot Wheels. They had bedrooms with desks, and striped rugby shirts and beds they slipped into a little past nine. And windows, shiny with the night.

The first time I left the house without my baby in tow was September, two months after our first child was born. We left together, my new husband and I. We went to La Ronde, the old Expo site. My first birthday as a mother. We left our infant with our friend Nora, who insisted we could not leave him with the two California hippies staying across the street, who'd offered, but might not know how. Who might not know better. Nora was a med student. She became a pediatrician.

The next time I left him was to give birth to our youngest. January. Six days in hospital. Six days on the obstetrical ward was standard practice to allow new mums recovery time, to have a break from housework, from the other kids. My first, now seventeen months old, stayed with his aunt and cousin and caught the flu, threw up all over his blanket whose name was "gulley gulley."

After I got home with our second baby, his father retrieved the oldest from his aunt's. It was 8 p.m. when they arrived at the front door and he stood, short and round in his red snowsuit, reluctant to enter. Holding his cleaned-up gulley gulley to his cheek, he wouldn't move. I coaxed him with his favourite ball, rolled it to him, urged him, kick the ball, love, kick it back to me. More than anything, he loved to kick that fat red ball. But he held out, sneaking peeks, calculating the risk, before the recollected joy of kicking the ball got the better of him. He lifted his small snow boot just a little when the ball stopped in front of his foot, nudged it back in my direction.

The next time I left was to go back to school. I needed two more degrees, a BSW and an MSW, so I could get a job. Make some money.

And then I left to go to work. To collect a salary, prove myself. I never could make as much as him. Not enough to make things equal.

And then June 28, 1980. I left with that suitcase. And returned every other week.

Paré

In 1983, I left again and did not go back. They lived with their father and I saw them some weekends, some lunches, some dinners. Their father wanted to sell the house. They were thirteen and fifteen then. I was thirty-six. My mother had died just days before.

Though no one called me names, or threatened me, still I was the one who had to leave. Out of all the possibilities, I was the one who had to choose absence, so we could all stay sane. No one can live for long tip-toeing over broken eggshells, a burial site. I left in stages. One day I left the house without them and did not go back.

My other shame: after three years of back and forth, I lost heart. After three years the house looked worn without a permanent parent to polish it full-time. After three years I thought they might be losing friends because of me, their lesbian mother. After three years they were adolescent boys. How much could I offer them? After three years I moved into a housing co-op. After three years my mother died.

When I told the kids I was moving out for good, my oldest put down his fork and said, You're not!

I lost touch with the day-to-day, the week-by-week, the parent-teacher meetings, their homework, their home from school, the talk at dinner, bedtime, the little day-to-days that made them who they are. I saw them regularly, they stayed with me sometimes. But they were growing up.

I let myself lose faith. In myself. In how much they might need me still.

I called him from our flat on Esplanade, both boys under three. He was working on a cardiac rotation at the hospital, a weekend shift. In the cone of street light out the second-storey window the snow fell thick as dandelion tufts.

I reached the switchboard operator, who transferred me to Cardiac, where I waited on hold for the head nurse, five minutes, who told me she would ask him to call me when he was free. Ten minutes later the telephone rang.

How come you're calling me at the hospital? He asked me as though he worked for the FBI.

You're going to have to come home right now, I said as reasonably as I could, making my voice sound reasonable, or I don't know what I'll do. The kids are in the bath, they're throwing water all over the floor. I can't make them stop. You've been at the hospital all weekend. I can't take it. It's Sunday, it's been snowing for days. I can't take another minute. Please. Come home right now.

He did not try to reason with me or talk me down. He said, I'll come home as soon as I can. Lots of patients in Emerg, we had a bad night last night.

So did I, I said, as calmly as I could, which by then wasn't very calm at all.

The Brothers Grimm began recording fairytales in the nineteenth century. They consulted no fairies. It's likely no fairies survived the eighteenth century. It's also likely the brothers did not believe in fairies. They inscribed the fairytales as they were recited by two local women. Story tellers, one of whom Wilhelm Grimm later married. The brothers changed some details that had been embedded in these stories for centuries. The bloodier ones. The Grimms wrote the stories for children, though originally they were as much for adults. Times were changing; it was hard to persuade parents to tell their children stories in which a ferocious wolf, for instance, rips a small girl limb from bloody limb. The grotesque was not nearly as popular in the nineteenth century as it had been in earlier times. The times of the witch burnings, for instance.

Even before the Brothers Grimm compiled these stories, illustrators had rebelled. They began to refuse to depict such grotesque brutality in children's books, despite the public's ongoing enjoyment of a public hanging. The illustrators softened the deaths in their illustrations, removing the more gruesome details. But those who died in fairytales, still died hard. An old woman burned to death in a fire set at the base of the tree where she was trying to hide. Of course, she might have been a witch. A girl died with her feet bleeding. She must have been too frivolous. Another woman died in a barrel, pierced through with knives, rolled into a river. A wicked woman — obviously.

↝

At the end of the second year, I weighed my chances of returning home without causing Hansel and Gretel mortal harm. Perhaps Fraq's curse would not survive his own death. But two women on foot with only a hunting knife and a little magic to protect them could come to some nasty ends.

We decided to travel as boys, fashioning trousers and caps to cover our hair. We left the Magyars when spring turned green. I didn't know what would happen with me and my family or me and Astrid or Astrid and my family, but I would not be parted from her.

We slept in trees and avoided thieves and priests. The countryside had been smothered in unholy smoke for so many years. Women, healers, heretics, witches burned, the smoke from their broken bodies after the stake perpetually in the air. We saw it. We saw it as boys, but we knew it was meant for us. I was a healer and had been away, a changeling, returning. Even in disguise, nothing could be presumed. Men too were burned. Who knows why. Priests and friars, like others who had power, were easily corrupted. Everything turned upside-down. In the village where I sold herbs and eggs, I was arrested. Recognized, even in my boy's disguise, by the village priest who found my trousers repugnant to the Lord.

I recognized the village men who led us to our make-shift cell. They gave us sacks to wear. They took clippings of our hair, checked under our nails, shone mirrors in our faces, bled our forearms into pans. The Judge agreed, the results confirmed that we were witches.

Paré

We'd been married more than three years when I challenged him to a fight. Bet I can beat you, I goaded, look at this muscle. I thought if I was sufficiently determined I could overpower him. Mind over matter. I had no brothers, and my sister was two years younger; I thought I could beat anyone.

I don't think so, he said, swooping me up and placing me carefully on my back on the sofa in the den. I could not believe it. I lay on my back speechless. I was not hurt. He'd picked me up as though I were a bag of wool — not even a bag of potatoes. And laid me on the sofa. On my back. He didn't even break a sweat or grunt or grimace.

How did you do that? I lay incredulous on the sofa. It had taken him half a minute.

He shrugged, didn't even crow, just how it was.

It shook my confidence. That day something inside me shifted a little. I still find it hard to come to grips with that kind of reality.

His oldest sister said, let's join the Consciousness Raising group at Susan's. It was January. I wore a navy blue sweater from the Army and Navy store over a blouse with a white collar. Crisp. And jeans. I did not look like a hippy that night; I looked determined. I was mad that we were not equal, that he could say, when you make as much money, we can both work part-time. And have that count as fair. That he could pick me up like a bag of wool.

Their eyes followed my footsteps
from the stove to the sink.   Those months
after.   When I left the room or answered
the phone or stood at the counter
spreading worry all over their toast.

The end is not the end; it leads on.
Opens up.   Opens like sutures or wings.
Maybe all children, even babies, must attend
their mother's footsteps.   They determine
which way the children will go.

~∂

A sparrow landed on my arm and offered us invisibility. How it entered the cell, I don't know. It was young. Its spell has been a little unpredictable, but it has lasted centuries. That morning we vanished, edging through the cell door after the guard. We heard his shouts as we raced through the village square and along the trail to my old cottage. The cottage was empty. We waited behind the woodshed, worried that the guards would find us. But, of course, we were invisible.

As evening fell I saw Heinrich trudging along the forest path, followed by a woman with large ears.

Husband, said the woman as they arrived at the cottage. She called him Husband!

Yes Wife, he replied.

Are you not satisfied we made the right decision? Is life not more pleasant without those pesky children squawking like baby birds. They troubled my ears. They will certainly be dead by now. Astrid had to hold me to keep me from falling over screaming.

Heinrich hunched his load of sticks off his shoulders, making a thunderous noise. He did not answer. The woman smiled to herself, humming like a hive of bees. We could see her face. I will make us a pudding, she said, with bread crumbs and a little honey. You will like it, she told him. Heinrich started. With honey? he asked. Where would you find such a treat?

I know some honey bees, she answered.

What about our children? he said, now we have more food?

Our children? she pulled back. *Your* children have no more need of food. They are in heaven where they belong. She led him by the hand through the cottage door, her ears glowing.

We watched the candles burn in the cottage windows until they snuffed them out, and the two inside put themselves to bed. Astrid slept that night but I could not. Fireflies lighted on her hands. They landed on white pebbles near the path, and on a button that once was stitched to Gretel's dress. I picked it up, a little button fashioned from a piece of bone.

We stayed. Heinrich and his new wife left by morning and returned by sunset. Every day, Astrid and I crept into the cottage that had once been my home. We ate what food we found, though in truth, there was not so much to eat. We ate cold porridge and scraps of bread, and honey from a jar underneath the bed. We slept on the bed.

When the other two returned, they saw evidence of ghosts wherever they looked. The kitchen was undone, the front door ajar, the bed, a rumpled heap. Food was missing. I refused to feel remorseful. I was not such a good woman. Nor was Astrid, who smeared a little honey on the bedstead and on the windowsill.

Soon the new wife refused to leave the cottage. To protect it, she said. She stayed alone in her kitchen, pounding chicken bones to flour and starting at every noise. When Heinrich returned, she told him she'd heard the children playing by the stream. Ghosts, she said, her hearing that acute. Every night she sobbed.

Heinrich arrived home one day just after the woman had lit a fire in the stove. She buzzed about, flapping flies away with her apron skirts. She called to him through the open door.

What did you say, Wife? he asked.

She sang out again, I'm going to have a baby.

Suddenly, I heard screaming. It could have been a wolf, or a bear with a thorn in its forepaw, or a fox in a trap. It came from somewhere in the forest. Only when Astrid placed her arm on my shoulder did I realize the screaming was my own. And then the woman started screaming too, frightened by my own screams. She ran from the house, her apron full of fire, flapping, her hair high with orange flames. We ran too, Astrid leading me down the path, hurrying, hurrying away.

Gudrun's thumbs rolled around each other, as though they were searching for a place to hide. Just the way my grandmother once did. She shuffled back to her room and closed the door.

I sat for awhile, then tidied up, put away the tea things. I baked cookies and made ice cream. When my boys flew through the back door after school that day, I caught them up in my arms as they landed in the kitchen.

But I lie: I did not make ice cream that day. Such a fantasy. Who has that kind of time? Enough to catch them in my arms.

After the thunder at the kitchen table, after they rose from their seats like little ghosts and stumbled outside again to play with Davey, after he looked at me like *happy now?*, I escaped into the bedroom and sat on the bed. I checked the mirror. I was still there. I looked around the room, at the dresser that had been mine since I was eight years old, now painted white, at the old plum tree scratching the side window, at the wallpaper and the white shag rug, at the night table with its surface now cleared of my bedside things. I wanted to rest for a moment in the silence of what was about to vanish before I slipped out the sliding door, unhinging my careful, careless past.

I might have said, if anyone had asked, this is the most important day of my life. The others, my sons, their father, would be shaped by this day, but I would be caught inside it. They were the tableau, it was being done to them. But I was the movement. It is the movement which bears responsibility. But no one asked the question, so I didn't answer. It seemed meaningful to be moving in a conscious direction, chosen, even though it was more by default.

The wallpaper was white, sprinkled with buttercups. In the past year, perhaps I'd seen too much of it.

Eggshells heap, clocks refuse, my hands semaphore love, a longing, suitcase blocking the kitchen door. The sun is suddenly released. It stands for nothing. Clouds flit like silent movies. I can tell that time is changing, becoming a dimension I can no longer count on. Inside the suitcase lies a shirt that memorizes future. Inside my pack, the bones of flightless birds, eggshells ground to sand. Inside the linen box underneath a pillowcase, shadows fold, re-fold like history, heavier than night. A photograph below the shadows: two boys with knotted ties and faces that look the camera in the eye, one a little formal, one a little clown. Inside a silver frame. The address on the door behind is 3665, first house they will remember. No shadow blacks the door. The bones are still their own. When I see the photograph it means everything is good, everything will fill with ache. When I place my shirt inside the temporary dresser drawer it means guard my heart. When I pour sand from the fingers of a glove it means regret. When I spread the shadow underneath the pillowcase it means begin to cry.

Pretend the sun can be a metaphor, that rain will only fall at night, that healing starts when the knife slides from the skin. It means look for bridges. Every house, another story. It means clocks tick forward only. Sun slides from clouds that ride like horses on an open field.

When I gather up the story of the mother who is gone it means button up my coat, it means open up my heart, it means one a little formal, one a little clown, a little in the camera's face. Continue counting blackbirds when the sun begins to bend. They've been left with their own father. He is not their mother. Keep picking up the photograph. Keep lifting up the suitcase from the kitchen floor. June is the month. It means am I sorry yet or a little bit afraid?

Paré

guilt: between my bones   years
           between my hands
           that open like a mouth
           giving up
           the middle hours of the night

shame: between my teeth and fitted sheets
           redemption on my upper lip
           tables   the kitchen floor
           between my shoulder blades
           while words like apple-
           juice and kick-the-ball
           catch like fish bones in my throat

grief: that too
           that too

I placed my suitcase and the desk lamp in the trunk of the car and returned to the house. To say good-bye. My oldest son slouched into the kitchen. Davey waited outside. I called again for my youngest son, but he didn't come. No one had seen him for the past half-hour. We looked everywhere for him, calling, calling. We looked under his bed, behind the sofa, in the hallway closet, the bathtub. Davey raced down the street shouting his name and knocking on the doors of other friends.

He had run away once or twice before, but we had not expected it this time. We looked behind the curtains and in the rafters of the carport. We looked in the basement and under the desk. We phoned the parents of his friends. We ran faster and faster, like moving fast would get him back faster. His father took a sandwich out to my replacement on the grass in the backyard. The mess in the kitchen mounting, but no one could stay inside to deal with it. We were everywhere else, calling my son's name.

After thirty minutes he finally appeared, prodigal, in the kitchen like a genie. He had been hiding in the laurel bushes out front, against the stucco wall, shaded from the noon-time sun, listening to us calling his name like a mantra. We were so relieved to see him, smiling despite the day. Hugging, hugging.

Then suddenly, there was nothing much to say. Nothing left. Everything was too important and could not be said. Only good-bye and I'll be back. Good-bye. A terrible thudding in the chest.

bones heave   lift from below the sink   and orange juice slides from its yellow jug   a pulpy mass   cupboard doors open/shut/open   torrents of clatter   forks and knives and spatulas   eggshells razoring the floor   dishes rain from shelves   soup spoons clank in open drawers   paper scraps and coins   matchbooks crayon stubs   turquoise beige and black   clutter in the counter corner   aprons   tea towels   gingham curtains torn

The heat one summer sizzled city birds roosting in the maple trees that lined the street. It manifested in wavy lines above the asphalt, the daytime air glassine. Nights he was at the hospital I filled the tub with cool water, sat in it when the heat broke through my sleep.

It has to break, said all the neighbour women on Esplanade, where we lived in a second-storey flat, above the Becks, below Mrs. Martiniuk, who owned the building.

This Montreal heat, it has to break, all the women said, wiping their brows with tea towels as I passed their stoops weekday mornings with a toddler in the stroller, an infant in my backpack, that overheated August. The afternoons, too hot to be outdoors.

Mrs. Martiniuk scolded me when she found our plastic garbage bags on the back balcony waiting for garbage day. The sun, she tsssked, shaking her head at my stupidity, it makes the maggots grow.

Most days we walked across Park Avenue, across McGill campus, to the Royal Victoria Hospital pool for medical staff and families. Some days we met their father there after he finished work, walking over from the hospital in his whites, kissing us. One day our oldest, who was only two, slipped into the pool silently, unobserved. Late afternoon, other families had left for dinner. The life guard was busy reading his newspaper and we were busy saying hello to each other. The quiet suddenly seemed eerie and we looked around. Our oldest had disappeared. The pool. His father reached down into the water and pulled him up to safety, held him upside down, all the chlorinated water spewing out of him.

The humidity broke when we got home that day. End of the month and after several rehearsals of thunder and heat-lightening, the rain finally fell in silver curtains, hissed into sidewalk cracks, drowning the yellow grass in little squares of lawn behind their rusting wrought-iron fences up and down the street. Every gutter was a new river running. We swarmed the street, all the neighbours on the block, men, women, children. We held our faces to the rolling sky, opened our palms to the flood, offered our babies to the broken, falling clouds.

127

Paré

My toddler calls me from the bathroom where he holds on to the seat with his chubby hands for balance, to keep from falling in. He's been in the bathroom for awhile.

Mum, Mum, he calls, newly toilet-trained, alone on the toilet.

Mum, come, though there is no panic in his voice. I push the door carefully, asking what he wants, this child balancing, full of new independence.

What he wants is this: Stay, he says, it's plain in here without you. So I stay.

How do we? Stay. With anything.

I stay with him that day. It's easy.

Harder in life's reckless movement. Harder to stay even with ourselves.

Speak praise for the ladybug.   Coleopterous insect
of the family Coccinellidae, who came one winter
                              when in my chest was caved a hole,
the size of a small fist.   Who came and stayed.   A gathering.
Twenty-four in the southwest angle of my ceiling, beaded
and rust-coloured.   A cluster, a small shield, a cloisonné clasp
the shape and size of a child's hand curled in.   Praise and gratitude.
Who came.   Bringing friendship in the mornings.
Evenings, too, when that space inside me wanted
something curious and watching.   Something that would not
leave.   Something come inside for winter.   To winter over,
huddle down and cloister.   Waiting.   Praiseful, waking to find
the small curve of ladybugs has not moved.   Has not abandoned.   Waits,
blood moon in the high corner above the southwest window.

They ate nothing, hurt nothing, they made no noise.
Glowed careful, cupped their wings.
They meditated, ate nothing.
                              How could they eat nothing?
                              All winter.
                              In the end
                              I didn't need an answer.

They died. Those ladybugs. Later. Months. I found them in the carpet pile or on my desk or in my shoe, red-domed husks, light as light. Fly away, fly away. In the end, one on the windowsill, sun through the ochre flake that had been its body. Its home. All praise and strangeness.

No houses were on fire. Light as light.
No children all alone.

That morning, the mess in the kitchen. Thinking a million miles an hour, telling myself: It'll be okay, it'll be fine, they're old enough. When I was their age I could take care of myself, take care of my sister too. They'll be fine without me round the clock.

I tablespoon the hours, live with it, act like it will be okay. Endure. Spoon out mouthfuls of my heart to satisfy divinities.

At thirteen, the bible says, Jesus told his mother not to worry about him, he had to be about his father's business. Is thirteen then the age? The official, sanctioned age, biblical, when children can manage with less mother.

Paré

When I left for the second time, three years later, leaving the arrangement of part-time parenting, my oldest, then almost fifteen, could not afford to be too much involved in anything adult, or even the appearance, but the look he cut across the table when he heard me say, I'm leaving the arrangement, was filled with disbelief. The awkward formality of the term, 'arrangement,' of the way I had to say it.

You're not! he said. The *You're not!* hanging in the air, out of his mouth before he knew he'd even thought it. It rang there long after he pulled his adolescent eyes back to his plate of spaghetti and meatballs. Kept them there.

The Blue Fairy

Everything is accurate. Everything made up. If I had more silence. If I'd never raised my voice. If instead, we'd moved into a duplex. Both halves. Two half-families. Two kitchens. Two sides to every story. If I'd had a perfect past, I would have reached a better future.

I breathe. Some nights I even sleep. I stopped going to confession long ago. Maybe my past was perfect. Everything as reachable as it can be.

After my mother died, she stayed inside my mind. She never goes away. Though she stays in the far background reaches of my mind, she's always there. An undertow. I know what she is doing there: waiting. Waiting for me to follow her out.

⤴

Three hundred years passed. Everyone I knew was dead, said Gudrun. I was as lonely as a red dwarf star. A woman approached me on the street in Dusseldorf, dressed in a blue gown. On her yellow hair, she wore a starred tiara.

This is true, Gudrun nods to me, when I raise my eyebrows in her direction. The whole story is completely true, she says.

Blue Fairy, I bowed to her. Gudrun continued, just a little miffed. I knew by the cut of her gown that she was a fairy. She carried her wand inside her sleeves. Always a give-away.

The Blue Fairy smiled. And you are Gudrun, mother of Hansel and Gretel, healer, seamstress, companion of Astrid, aerialist of the highest air. She spoke like that, old-fashioned, curvey. Do you know the story of your children? she asked me.

They died, I said.

She shook her head and began to tell me the famous fairytale. I'd been with circuses on the Steppes of Russia for decades, centuries really. Somehow, I knew the story of Pinocchio, but of my own children, not a word.

At first I plugged my ears. But she removed my hands. I hummed to drown her out, but she placed a finger on my lips. I closed my heart. I did not want to hear how they died. But she placed her wand over my heart. She waited while I cried. Then she told the famous fairytale of my children.

Listen, she instructed me, do not give up. You are a fairytale mother. One of the absent ones, whose absence makes way for story. Everywhere mothers leave, even if only for an afternoon. You will join Cinderella's mother and the mother of Snow White, the mother of Pinocchio, of Goldilocks, Red Riding Hood. From other places, other mothers too. From other kinds of stories, fables, novels, comic books. The mother of the Little Match Girl, Oliver Twist, Little Orphan Annie. You will work with them to make the world a kinder place, more understood. Your children search for you.

They are alive?

Did they not return in the fairytale, alive?

I myself should look for them, I say, wondering why I let the curse prevent me for so long. What kind of mother was I?

No, she said, a mother, who is of the past, cannot reach the children, who grow up into the future, but the children living in future, reaching back, can always find the mother. Watch and wait.

How will they find me?

In a kitchen.

How will they see me in a kitchen where I'm most invisible?

Make yourself visible. You are a mirrorist. Wear your mirrors; they will recognize themselves in you.

Gudrun lifts her arms. This is why I practise visibility in your kitchen. Both hands now. This is what fairytale means. Why I'm in your story. Understand, Schwesterherz, never to give up.

I begin to wonder if she's losing her ancient, romantic mind.

Even if it takes five hundred years. Even if it is cliché. I've lived long, and suffered, but I can almost feel my arms around them.

When a leaving takes place there is always the question: how? How did one thing lead to another thing and then another? Then away. How does it happen? How can the kitchen door slide open, the body be forced to follow through?

When, later, it feels all wrong, how does it stay unchanged?

the rules of the Fathers are buried
in the everyday   coded   knitted

into brows   purl-one-knit-one
                            my mother knit

the first set   sweater bonnet booties
a tiny pair of leggings   yellow

a neutral colour ... neutral
regarding the crucial question
baby boy   or would it be a girl

when he was born my mother
switched her wool
to blue   blue sweater
bonnet booties leggings   to reassure

in those days only three colours
were permitted
and two were sex-specific   I say

'those days'   but even now no one sees
a baby boy in pink.

The Infamous and Scandalous Trial of a Mother Who Became a Feminist Who Became a Lesbian (or Pat Robertson vs. Feminism)

The Charge:
Pat Robertson, former American TV evangelist and erstwhile-politician, has charged that "Feminism makes women leave their husbands, kill their children, practise witchcraft, destroy capitalism, and become lesbians."

The Defence:
Exhibit One: A Feminist (me).
> 1. True. I left my husband.
> 2. True. I became a lesbian.
> 3. False. I do not practise witchcraft — though I'm not opposed.
> 4. False. Although I mistrust Capitalism, I do nothing to destroy it.
> 5. False: I did not kill my children.

Exhibit Two: Two Children of a Feminist (my boys, now grown-up).
Remarkable exhibits: resilient, kind, thoughtful. Alive! (Crucial.) Who state they are able now to see life differently, with more compassion, because their mother (Exhibit One) became a lesbian. That's what they said. It was recorded. Remarkable children, positive, kind, always milking silver linings.

The Verdict:
Three out of five charges are unfounded.
Bang bang, twice the gavel falls: Not guilty.

Three years I came and went, as arranged, to and from the house where the kids lived and went to school, played soccer, ate dinner, watched cartoons in the basement. Every other week I packed my bags and came. Or went.

She's frail, but she could live forever. Now she claims she knew my great-great-aunt. What can I believe?

Truth is, I tell her, I never really leave them, never fall out of love with them. Am I too self-pitying? I ask her. Do I expose too much? Indulge too much?

She knits and mumbles over needles made of bone, clicks and clacks with fuzzy strands of white angora wool. Sometimes she answers me. All mothers are absent in the end, she repeats, which is unforgivable in this world. Every mother makes mistakes. Gudrun drops her needles, pulls out a row of stitches, begins again.

Some mothers tell stories. Some knit baby bonnets. Some sew, some practise enchantments. Many try to change the world. Some make zucchini pickles, twenty, thirty jars. What could possibly be indulgent in this realm? There is no bottom, nicht wahr? Keep breathing. Everyone lives a different life.

She stayed with me when I left altogether. After two more years she moved away. I missed chunks of their lives, I tell her when she visits, the at-home chunks. She knows exactly what I mean. I got weekend, telephone, birthday, and out-for-dinner restaurant chunks, I confess to her again, but not the day-to-day thirteen-to-sixteen, fifteen-to-eighteen-year-old chunks when they were making themselves into something they'd want to show the world. That part I missed. The domestic rug pulled out from under our everyday toes.

When I told him I was leaving, he said: you can't take the kids; I'm not the one who's leaving. Which is the rule: if you leave, you don't get to call the shots, take the kids. That much I knew. The one who leaves doesn't get to say or keep as much as the one who is left.

I dissolved into adolescence. Commercial radio stations played pop songs about my new in-love life. I had a new love, I had a new cause. I was in total head-over-heels holy righteous love. We wore T-shirts that proclaimed: *An army of lovers cannot fail.* One half of my life. The other half was my two boys. The third half was my full-time salaried work.

How to make it come out right? In the end, which is close now, it comes out only partly right. Though everything can change. Just like in the theatre: set changes may be minimal, but how the script changes, act to act, is significant. I took only a few things. Still, I took away my constancy, which is what I most regret.

End of day: sparrow song in a somewhere tree.
I keep watch at evening's window,
trying to think my way out, and into,
wondering where I belong. Even when my mother was alive,
life's uncertain edge. Alive, she was my walls.

I keep watch. The sun gives up again.
The sparrow, its series of repeated notes,
keeping the hour
from falling down around its head.

Evening keeps its promise, lowers itself,
the way the failing sun un-blues the sky,
the way the sparrow, silent now,
undoes the street, the way my mother …
The world will end.

The kitchen where I grew up. A dream one night. My mother just beyond the kitchen door, unseen, her voice lodged at the bottom of her throat. Dreaming is a way I keep her with me.

If my mother had packed her suitcase one Saturday in June, if she had announced, I'm leaving now …

Instead she warned: If you tell your father, I'll take a gun and shoot you. She already knew how much could be said against her, how much my father could accuse.

My father was a short man with a short temper, a ready joke, and a long list of hates. I never told him. Not because my mother would take a gun and shoot me, but because I never could assess how much of me he'd then need to hate. How much that hate would cost.

My former husband's father, my former father-in-law, later, years later, writes a note to me on a card. He tells me he found it in a desk drawer underneath a pile of papers, an old blank card with a black and white drawing on the front. He writes that he doesn't know what the drawing means, so he asks me to excuse the card, because the card itself, the sketch on the front, has no particular meaning.

Inside, he writes that he is sorry for the years he didn't understand, which catches me between the shoulder blades as I read his shaky blue handwriting. He is eighty-seven. That day, reading it, reading, *Sorry for the years, please excuse the card,* as though the card itself has been found unworthy. He apologizes for the card and for the years. I read it again. And then again. I keep it in my desk drawer underneath a pile of papers.

I knock on the door of the Vancouver bungalow I left thirty years ago. The house with the sliding back door. A woman answers, lets me in, lets me look around. In the kitchen everything gleams. No sign of mess or midden, the dip in the linoleum near the sink. The kitchen smells of lemons.

So it must be this: I am the midden. The heap of tears is me, mea culpas sliding down the side.

If you ask me, would you do it again, I would tell you yes. One or two things different. But, yes. Only those one or two things different to forgive then. Or three or four. But those one or two or three or four, they loom. I could have stayed another year or two, let them grow a little older than they were. I could have chosen to live closer to their neighbourhood. We could have all moved into a duplex, lived side by side. And when my youngest phoned from his father's house in distress, I could have told him to come on over. Devil in the details. How to forgive each one by one by one?

And my lover too. The one that lasts. I would do it again.
                    Her mouth is Greta Garbo, her skin is patterned on my lips.

Paré

Big mess in the house that Saturday. Nothing stayed in place. My youngest ran away and my oldest wore drooping eyes and my husband stood at the counter drying spoons. My suitcase waited at the back door and when the sun vanished behind a cloud I thought, *She'll have to come inside the house now*. But she didn't. She knew she had to wait outside until the mess settled. No one wants to clean up someone else's mess.

We looked and looked for him, my youngest who had run away. He had run away a few times before. Once for two hours. Once in Africa when he was only three he went missing for a full five minutes in a Nairobi shopping mall. We were in the bookstore when I looked around and didn't see him anywhere. The possibilities crowded in. He was so small and pretty. We looked in the shop beside the bookshop and in the central mall and I thought of the parking lot and all the cars, my mind crashing, and then someone brought him back to us. An older woman. Like magic, there he was.

We searched that day in June, our heads shifting right and left, made to come together as a family and call on his friends, be a group again because he had disappeared and, finally, it was his brother who found him in the shrubbery at the front of the house. Or did he just waltz into the kitchen, his feet cramped. The front of the house, a largely unused place we didn't think of. The front of the house that functioned as a facade for the neighbours with a tall rusting hedge and white pebbles instead of grass, and shrubs, green and red, to make a simple garden. Only company and the mailman used the front door. But he had crouched there behind a laurel bush against the stucco, waiting for the mess to clear. Waiting to appear again.

And then it was time for me to go. Finally, everyone just wanted the time of leaving to be over. Finally it was time for me to pack my suitcase in the car that I would bring back later so they could go to a movie in the evening. Their father thought a movie would be a way to get through the evening. *Peter Pan*.

The children rise into half-sunshine.   And their faces half fade.   Morning presses. Where are the words?   In their mother's mouth.   There is half-sun and half is cloud. All come together.   All split apart.   Morning presses down.   The red is plastic and the black is on the red.   The bowls are on the edge and the black is in the middle.   There is fading.   There is black in the middle.

When I thought of them in their beds that night without me to tuck them in, I had to make myself look away. The way I would have to make myself look away from my mother three years later in her hospital bed, dying, backing myself out of her hospital room, watching the last of her I'd ever see, her translucent waving hand, the top of her white angel-hair. I made myself turn slowly, walk, push the elevator button, leave for the airport to catch the plane home. Ottawa, home to Vancouver. I never saw her again. That day I knew I would never see her again. Walked away. All the while knowing. That's what we do. Make ourselves look away, walk away. I don't know how we do it.

The days go on without us if we don't.

I knew that when I saw my boys again everything would be shifted. I had placed myself in a new geography. Outside the white stucco. Beyond the cedar hedge.

These absent mothers mend and carry on. In absentia, they embroider kindness into coverlets and cushions made of silk, weave banners the length of the Autobahn. They stitch opalescent trances into the seams of overcoats, sew angel feathers into quilted vests. They festoon pillbox hats with shining discs. They hammer shirts of mail from the discarded claws of feral cats. Thread chicken bones and balls of foil, shadows on the threshold, binding hearts to fingertips, and fingertips to crayons, crayons to the Milky Way. Buttons out of bone. They emboss the sky with pennies flattened by commuter trains. Drape bunting in the towns. Every tent and tablecloth, garment, bedspread, flag and cape, bamboo or silk, each towel, each set of percale sheets, each shawl and scarf is laid right-side in and pressed. Smoothing out the wrinkles. Each slight and hurt, soothed, worries laid to rest.

On the other side of fairytale, the mothers sew dog stars into shirts, wolf intervals into brocade cloth, cockle shells to apron strings. Moon-rinds, diaphanous, grace stockings spider spun. They fold blankets made of moss and appliqué small tea towels with petals of real roses. Baste seed pearl words like care into belts and French berets. Paste semi-precious gems onto slippers made of glass and Findhorn ferns onto satin pantaloons. Sing harmonies, mend books and shakers of Dead Sea salt, transparent minnows, sea-churn from the Mariana Trench. Tack planets into orbits, knit one, purl one, repair black holes with tunes from *Pastoral*, the second act of *Norma*, Cole Porter, "Rhapsody in Blue," anything by Joni Mitchell.

Remember these mothers praising, chanting undersides, taking care of what is gone. Recycling what remains of good. Apologies into stockings, forgiveness into shoes. The tapestry. To blame or not to blame. The question: forgive or not. Yourself or anyone. Deserving. Everlasting choice. Who else will mend the grief? Cartoon squirrels fly into cartoon sunsets. The TV animates with timeless joy. All the lives within a child. Past, future, imperfect to infinity. Purl-one-knit-one. A starling leaves a maple branch, a somewhere sparrow sings evening into night. They join together fabric torn in two. They say all the words in order. They stir the soup, pour milk into glasses with pirates painted on the sides. A tooth is taken for a quarter. Bones returned to rightful limbs. All spoons spooning now inside their proper drawers, closed against the night. Snakes doze under beds. Supernovas and dwarf stars, the rings of Saturn spinning in their place. Expanding with every breath we take. Stars shift-shape the dust. A piece of you, a piece of me. Wish upon a page.

Everything's made up. Some things are true. I expect one day to inhabit light. I expect one day to leave these bones behind. One day find enough forgiveness. Cassiopeia blooms in the garden's outer limits. I expect one day to walk into my own heart, stumble into peace. I expect one day they will too. One day light will lullaby the sockets of our tired eyes. I expect to live among the meteors, suns, the hum of timelessness. Whatever all that is.

Between the first leaving and the second leaving, three years pass. Two leavings. We ate spaghetti with tomato sauce and meat balls. One of us cooked it. It could have been any one of us; by then we all cooked dinners like spaghetti and meatballs, chicken à la king, sponge cake with blue and purple icing. A family repertoire of simple family food the whole family knew how to cook.

When I said I wouldn't be keeping on with the half-time parenting arrangement the way I had for the past three years, that I would not be returning on a bi-monthly basis, they stopped eating. The oldest snapped me with his look. Betrayed a second time. His friends had stopped coming around. His mother was a lesbian. He did not betray me. But I betrayed. Again. At fifteen, I thought he needed friends more than he needed me. I was wrong. He needed me. But mother and lesbian did not fit together in that suburban neighbourhood. It made my sons stand out. I could not bear to let them bear it. But I was wrong.

Three years later, the second leaving was a bigger step. Before, I could still go back. But afterward I couldn't really. I didn't. I didn't much.

The unchangeable past is lost. Everything changed, buried in the marrow.

Bones buried in the midden, resting from the smite of life.

Don't be fooled. These are the facts. There are things I did not know, things I still don't know. I was also a good mother. There are things I cannot say. Objects in the rear-view are closer than they appear. Don't be fooled. I was strong. In the rear-view mirror, I am more faulty than I knew. I am not the person I used to be. Every seven years the body's cells rebuild and change. Since the day I left, I am fourth generation me.

They know the weight of sadness, these two young men sitting together on a sofa. My two Buddha sons, one the face of compassion, one the face of awareness. They sit in the ill-lit room, being video-taped by their aunt to use for the family counselling work she does.

We are better for it, they tell her, in answer to her question. Though what her question is I can't tell. In the video I see only my two sons. She sits off-camera, to the side.

Look, they tell her, we have more understanding now, we have more compassion, we are lucky. It was okay.

We learned more than we would have learned. They are letting me watch their copy of the video. I can see their young-man shapes, but whether their faces are smiling or sad or neutral, I can't tell at all.

Paré

heavier than she thought   the door
the way thunder racks the grooves

backyard wren on a hydro-wire
or a juvenile finch   house or rosy

too many wings inside her   now
she reverses flow

breathing just behind her septum
which deviates

the script requires flexibility   she does not
believe in hankies

always gravity   and charms against it
blue sky closer than it appears

the backward and the forward
the memory of home

thunders in her ears
the flow   the taste of iron filings

Before and after: how you think so well of yourself, think you are Pollyanna, until you do something wrong, something bad, unlike yourself, as you knew yourself to be. Which is the before. And then the after happens. You can never be before again.

My ten-year-old falling out of the cherry tree, falling directly out of it, another proof of gravity. His broken arm, dangling, angled like a compass in a high-school geometry set.

꙰

I find myself sitting at the kitchen table, which is strange, now that so much of it is over. The table in the old kitchen with the sliding back door, the table with the clear glass top. Gudrun sits beside me. She doesn't eat the borscht that glistens in her bowl. You are lucky, she says to me.

Maybe I am, I agree. I have only this ordinary lifetime, which is enough, not five hundred years, and my children, men now, still walk the city sidewalks, go to work, play tennis in the park. I visit them, hug them hello, good-bye. But for Gudrun, it's another story. For all her mirrors and silver thimbles, her canopies and shawls, for all the extra years the ancient spell heaps on her life, centuries now, she has never again held her children. She knows about the pebbles, the gingerbread, even the detail of the duck. Their faces, she wants to touch their cheeks again. Her children completely disappeared as though they were a trail of crumbs the birds had found.

I can see her, actually see the whole of her, even though this is a kitchen. Which alerts me. Is this a dream, or an altered state, an out-of-body sort of thing, a time warp? She hasn't visited for a long time, though she writes to me from wherever she's working. These day, she tells me, she's working with Snow White's mother and the Virgin Mary, hooking a fantastic lilac rug to restore the tar sands.

But here she is beside me now. The glass tabletop cold and solid beneath our elbows. Her oxblood boots, crossed left over right underneath the table. She tilts her head in my direction. You're worried, she says to me.

The mess in the kitchen, I suppose. How messes spread.

Ja, she says. You have your flattened penny, I have my button made of bone. We worry these small things, trying to fix something. Worry, worry. Fix, fix. I am certain, in the end something is going to change.

Open it, she nods, sliding a package in my direction. I unstick the tape, fold the wrapping on the table.

This black is the colour of the midnight sky and these studs are, I caress one, oh my, tiny silver birds. And mirrors like your dress! I kiss her cheek. The lining, tangerine satin, is embroidered with rosy finches all in flight, pansies and peonies. The shirt has no seams whatsoever. How did you do that? I ask her.

She winks, I do it for you. The black is for peace. The mirrors, for understanding. Stitched inside these sleeves, forgiveness for yourself. I made it with no seams so nothing untoward gets in. So nothing needed leaves.

I will wear it until I reach five hundred.

She smiles, It will last until you reach one thousand. You can wash it in the machine, dry it in the dryer. But only delicates, ja?

I try to hug her, but my arms don't fit around her anymore. She's more substantial now, visible. Something is changing. The kitchen begins to hum. Not an actual tune, more like a vibration, like the universe talking. And when I look at my hand, it's wavery, fragmented like a pixelated slide. Gudrun grips the table. The kitchen keeps on humming. Her little pipe rocks on the tabletop.

A thumping starts, feet on the stairs leading up to the deck, the sliding door. *Must be the kids home from school,* I think, even though the timing is way off. Years off. I stay in my chair and everything about me halts. Gudrun pushes her chair back, slow motion, rising slowly, her eyes on the sliding door. And there they are. A boy and a girl, wearing floppy blouses with round collars and wooden clogs on their feet. The girl's blouse is missing a button at the neck. Two birds hold up the ends of her flaxen pigtails with their beaks; a sparrow nests in the boy's blond thatch on top of his head.

My Leiblings, shouts Gudrun. The room stops, stops ticking, stops humming, stops pixelating. My breathing stops. Then the room rewinds, thrown into reverse: forks and knives lifting, flinging themselves from the kitchen floor back into their cutlery drawers, the spatula flipping a back-flip back into the frying pan, orange juice sucked back into the yellow jug, cupboard doors slam closed, and the floor between the sink and the stove buckles, heaves, eggshells and bones and dog-eared books, silver foil and carcasses of chickens fly up and vanish, then the kitchen levels, smoothing itself out. Three cereal boxes upright themselves, jostle into side-by-side formation, snapping to attention on the counter. Sheet lightning smears the ceiling, rolls around and around, then pours out through the open door.

Her children. A thunderbolt rumbles, spits, fizzles. The kitchen spirals backward in time. Everything quiet now and quietly crying. The room in perfect pitch. The three of them disappear, molecule by molecule, until their absence is complete. Underneath the table, side by side, her empty boots. Classic.

I rise with her soup bowl in my hands. I believe that in the midst of such occurrences it's best to clear the dishes. But no, I am holding a children's book in my hands instead, sitting in my own living room where I live with my beloved, on thirty years now, the one who looks like Greta Garbo, at least to me she looks like Greta Garbo, and who is right now at the grocery store buying milk and mandarins.

I'm sitting in my armchair, leafing through the story of Pinocchio, the illustrated version based on the Disney movie, which belongs to my grandsons, admiring the Blue Fairy smiling at Pinocchio, who looks, in this particular illustration, so much like his mother, all wooden, solid with potential.

The phone rings. I let it ring again — I screen my calls. But I already know I will answer it. It will be one of my children. What I'm always wishing for. Calling me. Just to say hello.

That's what happens in a fairytale. That's the way the endings work. Perfectly. That's the law.

I close the book.

Acknowledgements

Large and heartfelt gratitude to Shauna Paull, who helped initiate this project; to Betsy Warland, who read the manuscript at a pivotal time; to faculty, Lorna Crozier, Tim Lilburn, Lynne van Luven and students in the UVic Writing Program, who helped me shape some of my writing; to Patrick Lane, whose prompts and guidance fashioned a number of the poems; to the Fiction Bitches writing group, who critiqued the Gudrun story; to David Pimm, who provided German translations; to Ryan Rock for his terrific photography session; to Anne-Marie Bennett, editor extraordinaire, simply the very best; to Vici Johnstone for her extraordinary vision; to Chris Fox, first reader and supportive partner, who has always believed in the project; and finally to my two sons, who read it and approved.

About the Author

Photo Ryan Rock

Arleen Paré's novel, *Paper Trail*, was a finalist for the Dorothy Livesay BC Book Award and won the Victoria Butler Book Prize. Arleen has an MFA in poetry from the University of Victoria and her writing has appeared in a number of Canadian literary journals. Before beginning a career in writing, she worked for over two decades as a social worker in Vancouver. She now lives in Victoria with her partner, and has two sons and two grandsons.

About the Cover

Arleigh Wood
The piece depicted on the cover is called *The Great Escape* and is part of the "Cherry Blossoms Unfurl" series, which began while I was pregnant with my daughter. It seemed that pink and blossoms were everywhere I looked. I surrendered to the sweetness. Now I wait and watch the little tree grow. A flutter and a step into the unknown. Still the crow circles above.

The clever and mischievous crow comes out to play in my work. This dark bird represents the urban scavenger surviving and thriving on what the city has left behind. In my work, the crow can be seen as a self-portrait, a depiction of a creature living in both the urban world and one wishing to fly freely in pristine nature. It is in this place, where these two sides meet, that my artwork is born.

www.arleighwood.com
Photo Clayton Cooper

When she is not working in her Vancouver studio, Arleigh enjoys fast-paced urban explorations and peaceful natural escapes.